DAWN OF THE MESSIAH

AN EPIC RETELLING OF MATTHEW'S TESTAMENT

WWW.REKINDLEPUBLISH.COM

Copyright © 2023 Erick Lonzo

First Edition: December 2023

ISBN: 979-8-9893901-4-4 (ebook)
ISBN: 979-8-9893901-3-7 (Paperback)

Library of Congress Control Number: 2023922321

Published by:
Rekindle Publish
1501 W. Ninth Street #G
Upland, CA 91786

Cover design & Illustrations by Erick Alonzo

Printed in the United States of America.
www.rekindlepublish.com

REKINDLE
PUBLISH

DEDICATION

To Jesus Christ,
The true Author and Finisher of our faith,
The Alpha and Omega of every narrative,
For whom and through whom all things exist.
This work is but a reflection of Your eternal Word,
A humble attempt to echo the timeless tale You penned.
May it serve to glorify Your name and draw hearts closer to
You.
Amen.

ACKNOWLEDGMENTS

First and foremost, I'd like to extend my deepest gratitude to the cornerstone of my life, my wife, Sully. From the first glimmer of this idea to the very last word, your unwavering support, faith, and encouragement have been the wind beneath my wings. In those moments when doubt clouded my vision, your reassuring words and steadfast belief in me rekindled the flame. Your patience, love, and endless motivation have been pivotal in turning this dream into a reality.

I sincerely believe that behind every great endeavor is a source of inspiration and strength, and for me, that source has always been you. As we often say, we're a team, and this book is as much yours as it is mine.

To my dear Sully, may the Lord continue to bless you with wisdom and strength. With every sunrise, I find new reasons to love and cherish you. Thank you for being my rock, my confidante, and my biggest cheerleader. I love you.

DAWN
OF THE
MESSIAH

AN EPIC RETELLING OF
MATTHEW'S TESTAMENT

WWW.REKINDLEPUBLISH.COM

TABLE OF CONTENTS

PREFACE

Ever since I was a kid, I had this deep connection with the Bible. It wasn't just a book to me. It was the story of heroes and villains, of love and sacrifice, and most importantly, of a Savior who defied death. It's this passion for the Bible, mixed with a sprinkle of imagination, that got me thinking: How can I retell this incredible story in a way that's new and engaging?

Life is busy, and time often slips through our fingers like sand. I wondered how I could possibly find the hours and the right words to retell such an epic tale. That's when I stumbled upon an idea. Why not use modern technology? Today's AI tools can craft stories, answer questions, and even make jokes. But could they help retell the story of Jesus?

Let me be honest; it wasn't easy. Machines can produce words, but they can't feel emotions or experience the divine touch of spirituality. They don't know what it feels like to be moved by a verse or to have

their spirits lifted by a prayer. But that's where my love for the Bible stepped in. With a lot of prayer, meditation on His word, and some back-and-forth with the AI, we embarked on this unique journey together.

You're about to read the fruit of that journey. This book isn't just words and stories. It's an experience—a blend of age-old truths with a touch of modern tech. I hope as you dive into these pages, you'll feel the same love and excitement I felt while creating it. Remember, it's not just about the story; it's about the message it carries and the love it shares.

So, whether you're reading the Bible for the first time or the hundredth time, I pray this retelling brings you closer to Him. Enjoy the journey, and always remember the true Hero of our story.

ERICK ALONZO

INTRODUCTION

In every age and every culture, there are stories that transcend time. Narratives that are told and retold, resonating with each generation, finding new life and meaning in the hearts of its listeners. Among these timeless tales, there is one that stands unparalleled in its depth, impact, and transformative power—the story of Jesus Christ.

This book is not just another retelling. Instead, it is an exploration—a dive into the deeper layers of the tale, shedding light on its nuances and offering a fresh perspective on events that many might think they know. The aim has been to stay as true as possible to the original narrative while adding context, emotion, and detail to enrich the experience.

For some readers, this might be their first encounter with the life and teachings of Jesus. For others, it could be a familiar journey taken from a different path. But for everyone, it promises a tale of hope, redemption, and boundless love.

Whether you're a seeker, a believer, or simply a lover of good stories, I invite you to embark on this journey with an open heart. Let the words on these pages transport you back in time, to dusty roads, bustling markets, and the echoing lessons of a teacher who changed the world.

Dive in, immerse yourself, and let the greatest story ever told unfold anew.

PROLOGUE

Before the first stroke of a pen on paper, before the shaping of mountains and the formation of vast oceans, there was a narrative, a story woven deep within the very fabric of existence. It was a tale of redemption, of love so profound, and of sacrifice so immense that it would forever shape the course of history.

In a world veiled with mysteries and bound by time, there emerged a figure, both divine and human, a beacon of hope in the midst of despair. Jesus of Nazareth, the pivotal character in this narrative, lived in a time of great change and turmoil, a period that echoed the very heartbeats of prophecies whispered through the ages. His life, though recorded in ancient scrolls, resonates with the struggles, dreams, and hopes of every soul that treads the earth.

The Gospel of Matthew, an intricate mosaic of history, prophecy, and testimony, serves as the backbone of this retelling. Here, the words from dusty

pages come alive, painting vivid images of stormy seas, bustling marketplaces, and silent, starlit nights. The narrative delves deeper, seeking the human emotions and divine revelations behind every parable, every miracle, and every choice.

Yet, this is more than just a retelling. It is an exploration, an invitation to journey through familiar terrains with fresh eyes. To witness the world of two millennia ago, to feel the hopes and fears of its people, and to understand the timeless lessons they hold for us.

As you turn these pages, may you be transported back to those ancient paths, hear the rustling winds of Galilee, feel the palpable tension in the streets of Jerusalem, and, most importantly, experience the transformative power of love and grace.

In every word, in every nuance, may you find Him — the true Author of this eternal narrative.

Chapter 1

The Whispers of Prophecy

Under the Iron Fist: The Desperate Cry of Israel

It was an era of crushed spirits and lost hopes. The mighty Roman Empire, with its relentless grip, ruled the land of Israel. Its soldiers marched the streets with steely resolve, their armor reflecting both sunlight and the fear in the eyes of the Jews. But the oppression wasn't just from outside. Within the very walls of the temple, religious leaders draped in ornate garments took liberty with the sacred Law, adding layers upon layers of burdensome statutes. They, too, bound the people of God, but not with chains of iron; theirs were chains of tradition and legalism.

In the hushed corners of the markets, amidst the narrow alleys of Jerusalem, whispers of ancient prophecies flowed. The air was thick with expectation. "When will He come?" was the silent question burning in every heart. Every soul yearned for the Promised One—the savior who would liberate them from both their visible and invisible shackles.

The Royal Lineage:
Echoes from Abraham to Joseph

Once upon a time, in the ancient lands of Judea, there lived a young carpenter named Joseph. His lineage was royal, tracing back to the great King David and beyond, to the patriarch Abraham. This lineage was not just of blood, but of promises made by the Eternal One (Matthew 1:1).

As the evening sun painted the skies of Nazareth, Joseph, after a hard day's work, would often recollect the tales of his ancestors. He'd heard of Abraham, to whom it was said, "In thee shall all families of the earth be blessed" (Genesis 12:3). This promise, handed down from generation to generation, wove its way through Isaac, Jacob, and Judah, eventually reaching King David, the revered ruler of Israel (Matthew 1:2-6). David, a man after God's own heart, was given a promise that his kingdom would last forever (2 Samuel 7:12-16).

Yet, the path wasn't always golden. The lineage saw both heroes and scoundrels, both nobility and scandals. Through Solomon, Rehoboam, and Uzziah, down to Jotham, Ahaz, and Hezekiah, each story was a testament to God's enduring faithfulness (Matthew

1:7-10). The lineage meandered through times of prosperity, periods of exile, and moments of restoration until it reached Jeconiah and his kin during the Babylonian captivity (Matthew 1:11-12). The promise still lingered, even in foreign lands.

After the darkness of exile, rays of hope emerged as the line continued through Zerubbabel, Abiud, and Eliakim, winding its way to Joseph, the young carpenter of Nazareth (Matthew 1:13-16).

Joseph's heart swelled with humility every time he thought of his lineage. The stories weren't mere tales; they were reminders. They told of a promise - one of redemption and salvation. And as he prepared to wed Mary, little did he know that the culmination of that ancient promise was about to unfold through their lives.

Whispers of a Promise: The Divine Conception

The town of Nazareth was abuzz with the usual sounds of evening. As Joseph prepared for his impending marriage to Mary, his world was suddenly turned upside down. He discovered that his betrothed was with child (Matthew 1:18).

Whispers filled the air, and sideways glances were exchanged among the townspeople. The situation was scandalous by societal standards. Torn between love and tradition, Joseph's heart was heavy with sorrow. While the Law demanded one course of action, his love for Mary urged another. He decided to break off their engagement quietly, wanting to spare Mary from public shame (Matthew 1:19).

Yet, the designs of the Eternal One are beyond human understanding. In the stillness of one fateful night, an angel of the Lord appeared to Joseph in a dream. Radiating divine glory, the angel assured Joseph, saying, "Fear not to take unto thee Mary thy wife: for that which is conceived in her is of the Holy Ghost" (Matthew 1:20). The Savior, foretold by prophets and eagerly awaited by generations, was to be born through Mary. The angel proclaimed that the child should be named Jesus, for He would save His people from their sins (Matthew 1:21).

Awakening from the dream, the weight of its significance pressing upon him, Joseph remembered the words of the prophet Isaiah: "Behold, a virgin shall conceive, and bear a son, and shall call his name Immanuel" (Isaiah 7:14; Matthew 1:22-23). Immanuel, meaning "God with us," was a name echoing hope, salvation, and the close presence of the I AM.

Embracing his role in this divine plan, Joseph, with renewed determination and faith, took Mary as his wife. However, he honored her virginity until she gave birth to their promised son. And in obedience to the angel's directive, they named Him Jesus (Matthew 1:24-25). The Savior, the hope of Israel and all mankind, had arrived.

CHAPTER 2

THE STAR OF PROPHECY

Signs in the Sky: The Age-old Prophecy Unfolds

Throughout the great tapestry of history, the heavens have long been a source of fascination and wonder. Generations of stargazers have looked to the skies, hoping to decipher their mysteries. The birth of the promised Messiah was to be no ordinary event, and the heavens declared it so.

Ancient texts and prophecies spoke of this divine appointment. The Book of Numbers echoed with a messianic prophecy: "... A star will come out of Jacob; a scepter will rise out of Israel..." (Numbers 24:17). Genesis further affirmed this, mentioning a scepter belonging to Judah, likened unto a lion (Genesis 49: 8-10). And in Psalm 110, a decree stated the coming Messiah would follow the order of Melchizedek (Psalm 110:1-4).

To those familiar with celestial movements, this wasn't mere poetry. They recognized the symbolism in the alignment of stars.

Jupiter, known as "Zedek" in Hebrew, symbolized righteousness and had associations with the Messiah. On the Feast of Trumpets in 3 BC, Jupiter and Regiel (the brightest star in Leo, the lion) twined together in a helical rising, signaling the birth of the 'Righteous King' or 'Melchizedek'.

It wasn't just this alignment that was significant. As per Revelations, Virgo, representing the virgin, was clothed in the sun with the moon at her feet during this time (Revelation 12:1-5). The celestial scene seemed to mirror Mary's own circumstances, announcing the birth of the Savior.

Tales tell that Daniel, the revered prophet, had been privy to these prophecies and the profound signs they indicated. He had educated the Magi about these predictions, ensuring they were well-prepared for the momentous occasion. Aware of the impending birth, Daniel had even prepared gifts, symbolizing honor and reverence for the one who was to come. When the heavens finally revealed the awaited sign, the Magi embarked on their fateful journey, carrying with them Daniel's gifts and the weight of prophecy.

The Quest Begins: Magi from the East

Under a canopy of glittering stars, the vast expanse of the East buzzed with whispers of the celestial alignment. The Magi, learned stargazers and scholars, recognized the profound significance of the patterns forming above them. This wasn't just another night; this was the night the heavens danced in anticipation. Prophecies, handed down generations and etched in ancient scrolls, came alive before their very eyes: the birth of the King of the Jews. (Matthew 2:1-2)

Eager to witness this divine event, they embarked on a journey, following the guiding star toward Jerusalem. Dust billowed beneath their feet as the grandeur of Jerusalem's gates beckoned. Their singular question echoed in the halls of power, "Where is he that is born King of the Jews?" Their earnest quest for the newborn Messiah was more than just mere curiosity—it was a calling. (Matthew 2:3)

However, not all shared their enthusiasm. King Herod, upon hearing of another potential "king", felt a surge of jealousy and fear. The entire city sensed the tension. Cunningly, Herod summoned the city's scholars, demanding they reveal where the Messiah was prophesied to be born. The answer was clear:

Bethlehem, as foretold by Prophet Micah. (Matthew 2:4-6)

With a feigned reverence, Herod discreetly met the Magi. His voice dripped with faux admiration as he spoke of his desire to worship the newborn King. Instructing the Magi to return with the child's location, his dark intentions lurked beneath a mask of deceit. (Matthew 2:7-8)

The Star-led Journey to Bethlehem

The Magi, guided by the brilliant star, found their way to Bethlehem. The celestial body seemed to hover, its glow bathing a humble abode. As they entered, the sight of young Jesus with Mary overwhelmed them. The air was thick with reverence. Laying down their treasures of gold, frankincense, and myrrh, they paid homage to the one who was to change the course of history. (Matthew 2:9-11)

Yet, the divine had its own plans. Warned in a dream about Herod's nefarious intentions, the Magi chose a different route home, avoiding Jerusalem. Joseph, too, received a divine message, urging him to escape to Egypt with Mary and Jesus. (Matthew 2:12-14)

Back in Jerusalem, Herod's fury raged like a tempest. Feeling deceived by the Magi, he unleashed a torrent of violence upon Bethlehem, ordering the execution of innocent boys. The wails of mothers echoed through the land, fulfilling the grim prophecy of Jeremiah. (Matthew 2:16-18)

Time flowed on, and with Herod's eventual death, the danger waned. An angelic message prompted Joseph to return from Egypt. But upon learning that Herod's son, Archelaus, now ruled Judea, Joseph, heeding another divine dream, took his family to the quieter realms of Galilee, settling in Nazareth. This move, seemingly ordinary, fulfilled yet another prophecy, embedding Jesus' journey deeply within the tapestry of divine providence. (Matthew 2:19-23)

CHAPTER 3

THE VOICE IN THE WILDERNESS

In the gloomy shadows of King Herod's malevolent reign, the malicious decree resounded through the trembling streets of Bethlehem, seeking to extinguish the light of innocence from the city, one tender life at a time. Yet, amidst this darkness emerged a herald of hope, John, the son of Zechariah and Elizabeth. His birth, heralded by celestial whispers, was nothing short of miraculous. As King Herod's cold soldiers marched through the city with blades glinting mercilessly under the pale sun, a storm of terror loomed over the households.

In this storm of fear and bloodshed, Zechariah, laden with love and bound by faith, guided his wife and son to the wilderness' veiled sanctity. As Elizabeth nestled young John amidst the rugged terrain and the earnest warmth of her bosom, Zechariah met his end at the hands of Herod's merciless henchmen, his blood consecrating the sacred floors of the temple he served.

The tale of the hidden prophet, whispered amongst the faithful, swirled through the marketplaces and holy temples like

a mystical folklore, waiting to unfurl its essence upon the lands once again.

The Herald of the King

The Judean wilderness was an unforgiving expanse of rugged terrain, but amid its barrenness emerged a voice as robust and passionate as the prophet Isaiah had spoken of centuries prior (Isaiah 40:3). This voice belonged to John, clothed not in lavish robes but in camel's hair and a leather belt, a stark contrast to the finely attired priests of Jerusalem. His diet, too, was unique—locusts and wild honey, the sustenance of a man connected to his environment. He was known as John the Baptist. And his message? "Repent ye: for the Kingdom of Heaven is at hand." (Matthew 3:1-2)

John's fiery demeanor drew people from Jerusalem, Judea, and the regions around Jordan. They arrived in droves, driven by a mix of curiosity, conviction, and hope. As they confessed their sins, he baptized them in the waters of the Jordan River—a symbolic act, washing away their past and preparing them for the imminent arrival of the Messiah. (Matthew 3:5-6)

The Pharisees and Sadducees: A Warning

One day, as the sun blazed overhead, John noticed among the repentant a group of Pharisees and Sadducees. Their ornate robes were incongruous against the backdrop of the rugged wilderness. Their intentions were clear—they were there to scrutinize, not to repent. John, never one to mince words, called them out: "O generation of vipers, who hath warned you to flee from the wrath to come?" He challenged them to produce genuine repentance and cautioned against resting on their lineage, saying, "God is able of these stones to raise up children unto Abraham." The axe, John warned, was already at the root of the unfruitful trees, and every tree not bearing good fruit would be cast into the fire. (Matthew 3:7-10)

The Greater One Approaches

The atmosphere thickened with anticipation as John continued, "I indeed baptize you with water unto repentance: but he that cometh after me is mightier than I, whose shoes I am not worthy to bear: he shall baptize you with the Holy Ghost, and with fire." Here, John alluded to the one they all awaited— the Messiah. He painted a vivid picture of the Messiah's work, separating the wheat from the chaff, gathering the worthy, and burning the unworthy with unquenchable fire. (Matthew 3:11-12)

The Baptism of the Messiah

The very next day, as the golden hues of dawn painted the sky and the river murmured its gentle song, a figure approached from the distance. As he drew closer, John's eyes widened with recognition—it was Jesus of Nazareth. The moment was electric. The weight of prophecy and promise converged as Jesus approached John, requesting baptism.

John, feeling the enormity of the moment, hesitated, "I have need to be baptized of thee, and comest thou to me?" But Jesus, with calm authority, replied, "Let it happen this way for now, because it is the right

thing for us to do in order to fully do what is morally right."

With that, they waded into the Jordan. As John baptized Jesus, the heavens opened, and the Spirit of the Eternal One descended like a dove, alighting upon Jesus. Then, a voice, rich and resonant, echoed from the heavens, "This is my beloved Son, in whom I am well pleased." It was the voice of the I AM, the Eternal One, sealing the divine mission of Jesus. (Matthew 3:13-17)

CHAPTER 4

THE TEMPEST OF TEMPTATION

The Baptism of the Spirit

As the soothing droplets of Jordan cascaded down from the robes of the humble carpenter, the heavens themselves trembled in divine anticipation. Jesus, the embodiment of the Eternal One, stood amidst the earthly realm, His essence now united with the Holy Ghost as it descended like a gentle dove from the heavens. The celestial anointing, witnessed by the awestruck masses and the humble harbinger, John, was an awe-inducing scene that resonated through the eons. The young Messiah, now donned in the ethereal armor of the Holy Ghost, ventured into the wilderness that stretched beyond, its desolate vastness a reflection of the earthly desires and fears that veiled the hearts of men from the I AM.

The wilderness beckoned with a solemn allure, its barren expanse awaiting the footprints of the divine. With His earthly vessel, Jesus embraced the forty days and nights of fasting under the endless canvas of stars, as the nocturnal winds whispered

the ancient hymns of the Prophets through the skeletal branches of the sparse vegetation.

The Trial in the Wilderness

I n a vast expanse where the harsh sun cast long shadows on the sand, Jesus wandered, alone but with purpose. The wilderness around Him held stories of ancient times and whispered secrets carried by the winds. Driven by the Spirit, Jesus had come to this desolate land to fast and to commune with the I AM. Forty days and nights passed, with no food to sustain His body. His spirit was unbreakable, but His human form was on the brink of exhaustion. (Matthew 4:1-2)

Suddenly, as a mirage transforms the desert's view, the devil materialized, his eyes gleaming with malevolence and opportunity. "If you truly are the Son of God," he taunted, "command these stones to turn to bread." Jesus, drawing strength from the scriptures, replied, quoting Deuteronomy, "Man does not live by bread alone but by every word from the mouth of the Eternal One." (Matthew 4:3-4)

The devil, undeterred, transported Jesus atop the highest tower of Jerusalem. Gazing down at the dizzying heights, the tempter whispered, "If you're the Son of God, jump. For the angels will catch you."

Yet Jesus, ever steadfast, countered with another scripture, "You shall not test the Lord, your God." (Matthew 4:5-7)

In his final gambit, the devil showcased a vision of the world's splendors from a towering mountain. "All this can be yours," he promised, "if you kneel and worship me." But Jesus's spirit shone brighter, "Be gone, Satan! For it's written: Worship the Lord your God and serve only Him." Defeated, the devil vanished, and angels, luminous and gentle, descended, attending to Jesus's needs. (Matthew 4:8-11).

Light Dawns in Galilee

As news reached Jesus of John the Baptist's confinement, He embarked on a new journey, leaving behind Nazareth's familiar streets. He arrived in Capernaum, a city by the Sea of Galilee, alive with the buzz of trade and tales of seafarers. This shift in His path fulfilled ancient prophecies from Isaiah, signaling a great light dawning for people who dwelled in darkness. (Matthew 4:12-16)

With a voice that resonated with authority and wisdom, Jesus proclaimed, "Repent, for the Kingdom of Heaven approaches." Along the Galilean shores, He encountered Simon Peter and Andrew, fishermen

by trade. With a simple call, "Follow me," they left their former lives behind. The same call drew James and John, sons of Zebedee, into Jesus's fold. Together, they formed the beginnings of a group that would challenge the very fabric of their world. (Matthew 4:17-22)

The stories of Jesus's deeds, His profound teachings, and miraculous healings became the talk of distant lands. People, in their multitudes, brought the sick, the tormented, and the possessed to Him. He restored them, and with every miracle, His legend grew. Crowds from regions far and wide - from Galilee to Judea and beyond the Jordan - were drawn to this beacon of hope and light. (Matthew 4:23-25)

CHAPTER 5

THE
SERMON
OF
ETERNITIES

The Ascension of Teachings

Amidst the early morning mist, the hills of Galilee trembled with a quiet anticipation as the murmurs of a new dawn spread across the valleys and plains. The gentle whisper of a revolution carried the name of Jesus, the healer and the prophet, from lips to ears, weaving through the hearts of the hopeful. As the morning sun cast a tender glow on the mount, a great multitude gathered around the humble yet charismatic figure of Jesus, whose eyes held the calm of the heavens. It was on this mount he chose to reveal the eternal truths, it was here he chose to voice the echo of divinity.

The Beatitudes Unveiled

On the outskirts of Galilee, where rugged terrains ascended to touch the heavens, lay the Mount of Beatitudes. Here, a gentle wind whispered ancient tales, carrying with it the scent of the sea. Bathed in the warm golden embrace of the sun, a vast gathering formed, their hearts echoing with anticipation and hope. They had heard of a teacher who spoke not just with words, but with the very breath of the Eternal One.

Jesus, perceiving their thirst for knowledge, chose a prominent spot upon the mount. As His disciples drew close, the world seemed to pause, awaiting the divine wisdom about to be unveiled. In a voice that was both authoritative and tender, Jesus began, "Blessed are the poor in spirit: for theirs is the Kingdom of Heaven." (Matthew 5:3) The words held a promise, speaking directly to those who felt their spirits weighed down by life, offering them hope in the eternal kingdom.

He continued, weaving a tapestry of blessings and promises, "Blessed are they that mourn: for they shall be comforted." (Matthew 5:4) The weight of grief, loss, and sorrow felt by many suddenly seemed lighter, as the promise of comfort from the I AM resonated within them.

The air seemed to hum with divine energy as He proclaimed, "Blessed are the meek: for they shall inherit the earth." (Matthew 5:5) The often overlooked and undervalued found solace in the knowledge that their humility and gentleness were seen and would be rewarded.

A deeper yearning stirred within many as they heard, "Blessed are they which do hunger and thirst after righteousness: for they shall be filled." (Matthew 5:6) The seekers, the questioners, those who ardently desired to walk in righteousness felt seen, their innermost desire recognized.

"Blessed are the merciful: for they shall obtain mercy." (Matthew 5:7) A promise that rang true for all; for in showing mercy, one becomes a conduit of the Eternal One's compassion.

The wind seemed to carry His voice further as He declared, "Blessed are the pure in heart: for they shall see God." (Matthew 5:8) This was an invitation to introspection, a call to cultivate purity within, with the reward of beholding the I AM.

"Blessed are the peacemakers: for they shall be called the children of God." (Matthew 5:9) A declaration that extended beyond mere absence of conflict, speaking to those who actively sowed seeds of harmony and unity.

And finally, with a solemn undertone that hinted at the challenges to come, He stated, "Blessed are they which are persecuted for righteousness' sake: for theirs is the Kingdom of Heaven. Blessed are you, when men shall revile you, and persecute you, and shall say all manner of evil against you falsely, for my sake." (Matthew 5:10-12) It was a call to resilience and steadfastness, with the promise of the eternal kingdom for those who remained unyielding in their faith.

Pillars of Creation:
Earth's Salt and Heaven's Light

The sun, reaching its zenith, cast long shadows across the mount. The gathered masses leaned in, their hearts open, eager for more wisdom. Jesus, recognizing their hunger for truth, began with a metaphor both familiar and profound, "You are the salt of the world. But if that salt loses its flavor, how can it be made flavorful again? It becomes useless, only fit to be thrown away and trampled by others." (Matthew 5:13)

The imagery struck a chord. Salt, a valuable commodity in that era, was not just for flavor; it preserved, healed, and purified. By likening them to salt, He was calling upon them to be agents of preservation and healing in a decaying world. But the warning was clear: they must retain their essence, their 'saltiness', for without it, they'd be rendered ineffective, lost amidst the vast sands of time.

As the implications of being Earth's salt settled, Jesus introduced another metaphor, building upon the previous one. "You are the light of the world. A city that is set on a hill cannot be hid." (Matthew 5:14) Here, atop this mount, they were like that city. Visible, prominent. They were being called not just to shine, but to illuminate, guiding others through life's darkest hours.

And yet, with this great calling came responsibility. Jesus continued, drawing a picture with His words, "Neither do men light a candle, and put it under a bushel, but on a candlestick; and it gives light unto all that are in the house." (Matthew 5:15) Their light, their divine purpose, wasn't meant to be hidden or subdued. It was to be elevated, celebrated, shared, so that all might benefit from its radiant glow.

Then, with an intensity that seemed to pierce the very soul, He concluded, "Let your light so shine before men, that they may see your good works, and glorify your Father which is in heaven." (Matthew 5:16) This wasn't merely about them; it was about reflecting the Eternal One, the I AM. Through their deeds, through their very lives, they were to bring glory to the Creator, becoming living testaments to His boundless love and grace.

Timeless Decrees:
The Sacred Dance of Law and Heart

The wind whispered ancient secrets as it rustled through the trees. Before the crowd, Jesus, with a deep reverence in His eyes, began to address a topic close to the hearts of many: the Law. "Do not assume that I have come to abolish the law or the teachings of the prophets. I haven't come to abolish them, but to bring them to their full meaning and purpose." (Matthew 5:17)

Every word weighed with intention, He continued, "I assure you, until heaven and earth disappear, not the smallest letter or the least stroke of a pen will disappear from the law until everything has been accomplished." (Matthew 5:18) The Law wasn't just words on parchment. It was a living testament, a bridge between humanity and the Divine, the Eternal One, the I AM.

But as much as the Law was eternal, the heart's intentions mattered just as deeply. He ventured into the realm of human emotions, saying, "Whosoever is angry with his brother without a cause shall be in danger of the judgment." (Matthew 5:22) It wasn't just about the actions, but the very seeds of thoughts and emotions from which actions sprouted.

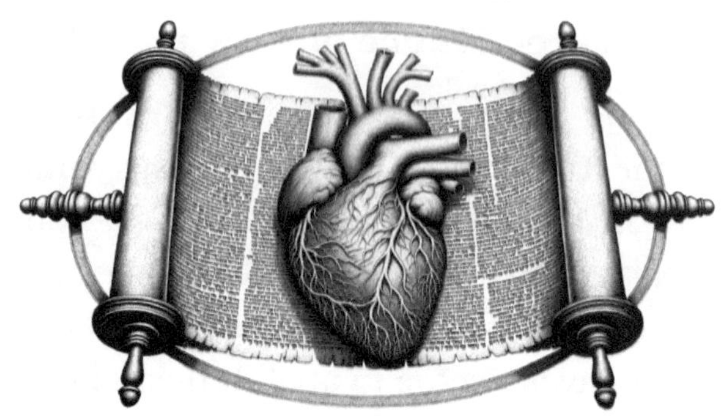

Drawing them deeper into introspection, He posed a situation, "Therefore if you bring your gift to the altar, and there you remember that your brother has something against you; Leave there your gift before the altar, and go your way; first be reconciled to your brother, and then come and offer your gift." (Matthew 5:23-24) The external act of worship and the internal state of one's heart were intrinsically linked. The grandeur of a temple or the magnitude of an offering paled in comparison to the simple, profound act of reconciliation.

The practical implications were clear. Settle disagreements swiftly, "Settle your differences with your opponent as soon as possible while you are still on the way to court together." (Matthew 5:25) For unresolved anger, like a smoldering ember, could flare up, leading one down a path of regret and entanglement.

With a solemnity that echoed the gravity of His words, He concluded this teaching, "I tell you the truth, you will not get out of there until you have paid every last penny." (Matthew 5:26) The journey of the spirit wasn't just about following rules. It was a sacred dance between adherence to the Law and the purity of one's heart, where true worship sprang from the harmonious union of both.

Echoes of the Heart:
Passion, Promises, and Purity

A hush spread over the gathered crowd as Jesus shifted the focus to matters of passion, commitment, and integrity. Every word was a gentle caress, yet an urging call, beckoning them to the highest realms of inner purity.

"You have heard that it was said by them of old time, 'You shalt not commit adultery'." (Matthew 5:27) His voice resounded with the gravity of ancient teachings. "But I say unto you, That whosoever looks on a woman to lust after her has committed adultery with her already in his heart." (Matthew 5:28) The listeners could feel it — it wasn't just the act, but the very seed of thought that mattered. The heart's whispers were as profound as the shouts of actions.

Gesturing with a fervor that mirrored the intensity of His words, He continued, "If your right eye causes you to stumble, remove it and get rid of it." (Matthew 5:29) It wasn't a call for literal self-mutilation but a passionate urging to rid oneself of anything that stands as a hindrance to one's spiritual journey.

Turning the page, Jesus delved into the covenant of marriage, an institution revered and treasured. "It has been said, Anyone who wishes to divorce his wife should provide her with a formal divorce document." (Matthew 5:31) But with the gravity that only the Son of God could carry, He added, "But I say unto you, Anyone who divorces his wife, except in cases of sexual immorality, causes her to commit adultery." (Matthew 5:32) Every bond was sacred, every commitment a mirror of divine covenants.

The teachings flowed seamlessly into the realm of speech and promises. "Again, you have heard that it hath been said by them of old time, 'Do not make false promises or oaths, but fulfill the commitments you make to the Lord'." (Matthew 5:33) The air grew dense with anticipation as He stated, "But I tell you, don't swear at all, not by heaven (because it's God's throne) or by the earth (because it's His footstool)... Instead, let your words be simple 'yes' or 'no,' for anything more than that is rooted in evil doing." (Matthew 5:34-37)

In the heart of these teachings was a call to sincerity, purity, and absolute commitment. The essence was clear: Rise above, strive for purity in thought and deed, and anchor oneself in the unwavering integrity of heart and soul. The Eternal One, the I AM, beckoned them closer to a life of sacred harmony and profound depth.

Whispers of Celestial Love: Rising Beyond Revenge

As the sun cast its golden glow over the hills, shadows danced, hinting at battles of old and of moral confrontations that have stood the test of time. With a gaze that saw beyond the horizon, Jesus navigated the hearts of the crowd to the realms of divine love and supreme forgiveness.

"You have heard that it was said, 'An eye for an eye, and a tooth for a tooth'." (Matthew 5:38) His voice echoed the age-old codes of retribution. "But I tell you, don't retaliate against evil. If someone strikes you on the right cheek, offer them the other one as well." (Matthew 5:39) This was not a call to pacifism but a profound challenge to transcend the desire for

revenge, to find strength in vulnerability, and to conquer hatred with love.

Guiding them further into the labyrinth of human interactions, He continued, "If someone sues you in court and takes your coat, give them your cloak as well. And if someone forces you to go one mile, go with them for two miles." (Matthew 5:40-41) These words were not just principles but an invitation to a higher life – a life that mirrored the magnanimity of the heavens.

The teachings turned even more radical. "Give to those who ask, and don't turn away from those who wish to borrow from you." (Matthew 5:42) In a world of transactional exchanges, this was the path of unbounded generosity.

Yet, the climax of His discourse soared even higher, touching the very essence of divine nature. "You have heard that it was said, 'Love your neighbor and hate your enemy.' But I tell you, love your enemies, bless those who curse you, do good to those who hate you, and pray for those who mistreat you and persecute you" (Matthew 5:43-44)

The profound reason was unveiled, "This way, you will demonstrate that you are the true children of your Heavenly Father, because He causes the sun to rise on both the wicked and the righteous, and sends rain to benefit both the just and the unjust." (Matthew 5:45) This was the heart of the matter – to reflect the indiscriminate and boundless love of the Eternal One, the I AM.

Closing this divine revelation, Jesus brought it full circle, "So strive to be complete, just as your Heavenly Father is complete." (Matthew 5:48) Perfection was not a distant ideal, but a journey towards boundless love and celestial wisdom. The path was clear, and the journey epic, as the listeners were beckoned to walk in the footsteps of the Divine.

CHAPTER 6

THE SACRED VEIL UNVEILED

As the sun climbed higher in the firmament, casting a divine glow on the olive trees that adorned the Mount of Beatitudes, the souls gathered around Jesus felt a wave of holy anticipation sweeping over them. The Sermon on the Mount continued, each word from Jesus was like a droplet of divine wisdom quenching the spiritual thirst of the multitude. The followers sat in an almost celestial serenity, their hearts fluttering like leaves in a gentle breeze with every word that Jesus uttered. The world seemed to stand still as he delved into the intricacies of prayer, revealing the sanctity that envelopes it.

Echoes in Silence: The Sacred Art of Giving

On a day radiant with divine purpose, the mountaintop where he had previously shared profound truths once again became the epicenter of wisdom. The backdrop of nature, birds fluttering and leaves rustling, seemed to lean in, hungry for the wisdom that would soon flow.

From where he stood, surveying the multitude before him, Jesus, His eyes deep pools of ancient knowledge, began, "Be cautious not to display your acts of kindness in front of others to gain their approval; otherwise, you won't receive a reward from your Heavenly Father." (Matthew 6:1) These words were audacious,

challenging deep-seated traditions, reshaping perceptions of genuine generosity.

Suddenly, a distant trumpet sounded. To the crowd, it might have seemed like a routine call, but in that sacred atmosphere, its significance transformed. "When you give to those in need," Jesus continued, masterfully tying the sound of the trumpet to the essence of his message, "don't make a big show of it like the hypocrites who seek the praise of others. Their reward? Temporary and empty applause from the crowd." (Matthew 6:2)

Murmurs rippled through the gathering. Many had witnessed such flamboyant acts of giving, where the intention behind the act became questionable. But here, Jesus was drawing a picture of true sanctity, suggesting that genuine charity was a sacred dance with the Eternal One.

His final words on the matter carried a purity and depth: "But when you give to those in need, do it so discreetly and intimately that even your left hand doesn't know what your right hand is doing. Make your selfless act a silent offering to the universe. And rest assured, the Father, the I AM, who observes the hidden, the quiet intentions and deeds, will reward you openly." (Matthew 6:3-4)

The truth of his message, echoing in its profound simplicity, found its way into the hearts of those present. The act of giving was transformed, moving away from spectacle, and becoming instead a silent, profound declaration of genuine love and selflessness.

Whispers to the Heavens:
The Sanctum of Communion

As the vast horizon painted a myriad of colors against the backdrop of a receding sun, the gathering around Jesus began to swell, each soul drawn to the profound resonance of His words. The air, previously filled with the hum of daily routines, now seemed to halt, becoming a serene oasis where souls would quench their thirst for divine truths.

He continued, steering the attention to another integral facet of their spiritual practice. "When you pray," He began, voice deep like the resonating echo of a temple bell, "do not be as the hypocrites who love to pray standing in the synagogues or on street corners, for they wish only to be seen by men. They wear their piety as a mask, and in that fleeting recognition, they find their only reward." (Matthew 6:5)

Silence ensued, interrupted only by the distant murmur of the evening winds. He prompted them to visualize an alternative, "But when you wish to commune with the Eternal One, enter into your inner sanctum, your chamber, and shut the world out. In that quiet, let your soul reach out to the I AM. And He, who sees the unseen, will reward you in ways you've yet to fathom." (Matthew 6:6)

As the audience reflected, some closing their eyes, imagining this sacred communion, Jesus offered them a prayer, one that transcended rituals and reached straight into the heart of divine connection. "After this manner, therefore, pray: Our Father which art in heaven, Hallowed be thy name. Thy kingdom come. Thy will be done in earth, as it is in heaven. Give us this day our daily bread. And forgive us our debts, as we forgive our debtors. And lead us not into temptation, but deliver us from evil: For thine is the kingdom, and the power, and the glory, forever. Amen." (Matthew 6:9-13)

The words flowed like a river, reaching into the very depths of their souls. But Jesus, sensing the weight of forgiveness in the hearts of many, continued, "If you forgive others their transgressions, your Heavenly Father will also forgive you. But if you withhold forgiveness, how can you expect to receive it from the I AM?" (Matthew 6:14-15)

The message of forgiveness hung heavy in the air. Transitioning to the sacred act of fasting, Jesus urged, "When you fast, do not wear a somber face like the hypocrites. They disfigure their faces to be recognized by men. Yet, their reward is nothing but a fleeting acknowledgment." (Matthew 6:16)

He offered a sacred alternative, "Instead, anoint your head, wash your face, and let not your fast be known unto men, but unto the Father. And the Eternal One, the beholder of secrets, shall reward you openly." (Matthew 6:17-18)

The revelation was illuminating. True spiritual acts, whether prayer or fasting, were intimate dialogues between the soul and the Divine, devoid of pretense or the need for worldly validation. They were the echoes of a heart in pursuit of eternity, heard only by the heavens.

The Eternal Horizon: Unveiling the Heart's True Luminescence

In the midst of tranquility, Jesus' gaze lifted toward the heavens, effortlessly drawing all eyes to the vast expanse above. His words began to weave a tapestry of wisdom through the enraptured assembly.

He imparted, "Lay not up for yourselves treasures upon earth, where moth and rust corrupt, and where thieves break through and steal." (Matthew 6:19) The words resounded with an eternal weight, painting visions of fleeting earthly riches and the transience of material wealth.

He continued, "But lay up for yourselves treasures in heaven, where neither moth nor rust corrupt, and where thieves do not break through nor steal." (Matthew 6:20) The notion of an eternal, incorruptible treasure stirred the spirits of those who listened, each heart pondering upon the treasures that awaited beyond the earthly realm.

As eyes twinkled with newfound understanding, Jesus offered a profound truth, "For where your treasure is, there will your heart be also." (Matthew 6:21) A hush fell upon the multitude, as if each soul were traversing into the chambers of their hearts, evaluating the treasures concealed therein.

In the gentle caress of the evening zephyr, the Master illuminated deeper, "The light within you is your vision: if your vision is singular and pure, your entire being will be bathed in radiant light" (Matthew 6:22) As if the night itself held its breath, the assembly pondered on the light, understanding that the purity of intent enables one to walk in divine illumination.

Yet, He warned, "But if your vision is clouded with darkness, your whole being will be shrouded in shadows. If the light within you turns to darkness, oh, how profound that darkness becomes!" (Matthew 6:23) The wisdom cascaded like a gentle stream through hearts, revealing that the perspective from which they viewed the world around them, whether in light or darkness, shaped their inner being.

Gently, He drew their hearts towards a pivotal choice, "No one can be devoted to two masters, for they will either cherish one and resent the other, or cling to one and reject the other. You cannot pledge your allegiance to both God and material wealth." (Matthew 6:24)

It was as though time itself stood still. Every listener, now introspective, found themselves on the precipice of eternal choices, betwixt transient treasures and the eternal glory of serving the I AM.

Thus, with the heavenly firmament as a testament, the message echoed into the expanse: the treasures of the heart illuminate one's path, and in the luminosity of pure, undivided service to the Eternal One, true riches are found.

Dance of the Sparrows:
The Unfaltering Symphony of Trust

"So I tell you, do not worry about your life, about what you shall eat or drink, or even what to clothe your body with." (Matthew 6:25) The weight of worldly anxieties seemed to momentarily lift as His words permeated the air, invoking contemplation among His listeners.

Drawing their attention to nature's splendor, He continued, "Isn't life itself greater than sustenance, and the body more than clothing? Look at the birds in the sky: they don't sow, reap, or gather into storehouses, yet your Heavenly Father provides for them." (Matthew 6:26) The wind gently carried the distant trills of birds, underscoring His words and making the message intimate and tangible.

Gazing intently at them, He questioned, "Are ye not much better than they?" (Matthew 6:26b) A profound silence enveloped the gathering, the very air pregnant with revelation.

He pursued the core of their innermost fears, "Which of you by taking thought can add one cubit unto his stature?" (Matthew 6:27) The futility of worry was laid bare, as they contemplated the limitations of their own power.

"Why worry about clothing?" He mused, allowing His words to paint a vivid picture before them. "Consider the lilies of the field, how they grow; they toil not, neither do they spin. Yet I say unto you, that even Solomon in all his glory was not arrayed like one of these." (Matthew 6:28-29)

With a voice filled with warmth and compassion, He asserted, "If God adorns the grass of the field, which exists today and is gone tomorrow, won't He much more provide for you, O you of little faith?" (Matthew 6:30)

He beckoned them to a higher perspective, away from the tumult of worldly concerns. "So, do not fret over what you shall eat, drink, or wear, for these are the concerns of the world." He paused, letting the weight of the realization settle. "Instead, prioritize seeking the Kingdom of God and His righteousness; and all these things shall be granted unto you." (Matthew 6:31-33)

As the stars began their celestial dance, He imparted one final, timeless piece of wisdom, "Therefore, worry not for tomorrow, for tomorrow shall worry about its own things. Each day has enough trouble of its own." (Matthew 6:34)

The words resonated like a lullaby in their hearts, reminding them of the boundless love and care of the Eternal One. The Dance of the Sparrows echoed the grand symphony of trust, a melody inviting all to partake in the unfathomable peace of relying wholly on the I AM.

CHAPTER 7

REFLECTIONS OF HEAVEN'S LIGHT

Dusk's Sacred Echoes

As the soft whispers of dusk approached the boundless plains, the world seemed to hush its clamor, drawing its essence towards the heart of heavenly wisdom nestled atop the mount. The gentle lull of the evening brought no discontent, as hunger and weariness were forgotten amid the treasure of celestial knowledge unfolding. The disciples, along with the vast multitude, sat enraptured as the veil between the heavens and the earth seemed to thin with every utterance from the lips of Jesus. The earthly realm seemingly intertwined with the divine as the sun cast a soft golden glow, heralding the profound continuance of the Sermon on the Mount.

The Mirror of Self-Reflection: Beyond the Surface of Judgment

The sun stood high, casting long shadows upon the ground as the listeners hung on to every word spoken by Jesus. A gentle breeze rustled through the trees, carrying with it whispers of wisdom and tales of old.

"Do not judge, or you too will be judged," Jesus began, his eyes scanning the crowd, ensuring his message reached every soul. (Matthew 7:1) His voice, soft yet commanding, conveyed the weight of the principle he was about to unravel.

"With the same judgment you pronounce, you will be judged; and with the measure you use, it will be measured to you," He continued, emphasizing the reciprocative nature of judgment. (Matthew 7:2)

Drawing them further into the heart of the matter, Jesus painted a vivid picture. "Why do you look at the speck in your brother's eye, but fail to notice the beam in your own eye?" (Matthew 7:3) He paused, allowing the imagery to sink deep into their hearts.

The murmurings among the crowd grew louder, the discomfort palpable. Jesus' words were piercing through layers of self-deception, challenging their perceptions.

"How can you say to your brother, 'Let me take the speck out of your eye,' while there is still a beam in your own eye?" He pressed on, addressing the hypocrisy often masked by righteous intentions. (Matthew 7:4)

With profound compassion, He offered them the path to true discernment. "First, remove the beam from your own eye, and then you will see clearly to remove the speck from your brother's eye." (Matthew 7:5) This was not a call to abandon discernment but to engage it with self-awareness and humility.

As His teachings often did, Jesus provided a word of caution, further illustrating the importance of discernment. "Do not give dogs what is sacred; do not throw your pearls to pigs. If you do, they may trample them under their feet, and then turn and tear you to pieces." (Matthew 7:6)

The weight of the message hung in the air. The call to introspection was clear. The Mirror of Self-Reflection was placed before each soul, urging them to peer beyond the surface, to see beyond judgments, and to tread the path of wisdom under the watchful eyes of the Eternal One.

Seeking the Divine:
The Dance of Prayer and the Rule of Gold

The atmosphere atop the mountaintop remained charged with rapt attention as Jesus transitioned into a topic so essential to the human experience: prayer. Birds continued their songs, and the gentle breeze whispered its assent, as if all of creation paused to consider the profound teachings to come.

With a voice resonant and sure, Jesus beckoned the audience deeper into the mystery of the Divine. "Ask, and you shall receive; seek, and you shall discover; knock, and the door shall swing wide open for you." (Matthew 7:7) This call was not merely an invitation but a promise. The act of asking, seeking, and knocking reflected a spiritual journey—one that invited believers into an intimate relationship with the I AM.

He continued, painting a vivid picture, "For anyone who asks, shall receive; and the seeker shall find; and to the one who knocks, the door shall swing open." (Matthew 7:8) As parents respond to the cries and needs of their children, so does the Eternal One to His beloved creation.

Seeking to drive home the message, Jesus drew a parallel, "Or what man is there of you, whom if his son ask bread, will he give him a stone? Or if he ask a fish, will he give him a serpent?" (Matthew 7:9-10) It was a poignant reminder of the goodness of God—a Father infinitely more compassionate and generous than earthly parents.

Knowing that understanding often stems from relatability, Jesus appealed to their innate sense of compassion: "If ye then, being evil, know how to give good gifts unto your children, how much more shall your Father which is in heaven give good things to them that ask him?" (Matthew 7:11) The comparison was stark, illuminating the boundless, immeasurable love of the Eternal One.

And then, like the crescendo in a symphony, Jesus introduced a rule—a principle that would become the bedrock of ethical conduct across ages. "So treat others as you would want them to treat you, for this encapsulates the essence of the law and the teachings of the prophets." (Matthew 7:12) The Golden Rule, as it would later be termed, was not merely about reciprocity; it was the manifestation of divine love, a call to mirror God's heart in interactions with one another.

The implications of this teaching would echo across time, challenging believers to align their actions with their intentions and to see in every face, friend or foe, a reflection of the Divine.

Between Two Realms:
The Saga of the Narrow Door

Jesus, fully aware of the weight of His next teaching, let His gaze sweep across the sea of faces, as if peering into the depths of each soul. "Enter through the narrow gate," He began, his voice bearing both a warning and an invitation, "because the gate is wide

and the road is broad that leads to destruction, and many choose that path." (Matthew 7:13)

A ripple of unease ran through the crowd. They were all too familiar with the vast and tempting roads of life, paved with transient joys and fleeting satisfactions. These were the paths of least resistance, where the soul was lulled into complacency, unaware of the lurking dangers.

Seeing the deep contemplation in their eyes, Jesus continued, "But the gate is narrow, and the path is demanding, leading to life, and only a few discover it." (Matthew 7:14) The word "life" hung in the air, not merely hinting at existence, but a life of purpose, connection, and eternal significance. The narrow door was not a mere entryway; it represented a conscious choice, a decision to embark on a journey less trodden, one of sacrifice, love, and unyielding faith in the Eternal One.

The stark contrast between the two gates was not lost on the listeners. The imagery was vivid: one vast and welcoming, promising immediate pleasures but leading to unforeseen perils, and the other, narrow and demanding, yet opening up to vistas of eternal beauty and profound joy.

The message was a call to introspection, to examine the paths each had chosen in their lives, and to seek the way that resonated with the deepest truths of existence. It was a beckoning towards a journey, not just of distance, but of depth and discovery, where each step taken towards the narrow door was a step closer to the heart of the I AM.

Echoes of Destiny:
The Symphony of True Nature

Drawing them back from their reflections on the two gates, Jesus issued a caution that bore the gravity of ages, "Beware of false prophets," He warned, his voice deep and resonant, "who come to you in sheep's clothing, but inwardly they are ravenous wolves." (Matthew 7:15)

Murmurs of apprehension swept through the crowd. They lived in an era where spiritual leaders held significant sway, guiding the masses with their teachings. The imagery of a wolf, cunning and deceptive, hiding under the guise of an innocent sheep was both disturbing and enlightening. They had encountered such beings, those who professed piety but harbored malice and self-interest.

Sensing their unease, Jesus offered a touchstone for discernment, "Ye shall know them by their fruits." He declared. "Do men gather grapes of thorns, or figs of thistles?" (Matthew 7:16) The analogy was clear, simple, yet deeply profound. Just as a tree is recognized by the fruit it bears, so too would the true nature of a person, or prophet, be revealed by their actions and the impact they left behind.

Taking a moment to let the analogy sink in, He continued, "Just as a good tree bears good fruit, a corrupted tree yields bad fruit. A good tree cannot produce bad fruit, nor can a corrupted tree bear good fruit." (Matthew 7:17-18) The order of the universe, the divine design, was immutable. Authenticity, integrity, and true nature could not be hidden for long. The essence of a being would inevitably shine through, revealing either the light of the Eternal One or the shadows of deceit.

With a finality that left no room for doubt, Jesus declared, "Any tree that fails to bear good fruit is cut down and thrown into the fire. Therefore, you shall recognize them by their fruits." (Matthew 7:19-20)

The teaching was a clarion call for discernment and vigilance. It served as a reminder that appearances could be deceptive, and that true wisdom lay in observing, understanding, and recognizing the fruits of one's actions. For in this symphony of existence, it was these fruits that echoed the true nature of a soul, harmonizing with the grand design of the I AM.

Foundations of the Soul

The atmosphere had taken on an electrifying intensity. The vast sea of faces, each bearing the marks of life's tribulations and joys, now hung onto every word Jesus spoke. The breeze seemed to hold its breath, carrying with it only the profound teachings of the man who stood in their midst, a bridge between the heavens and the earth.

With a gravity that demanded the full attention of every soul present, Jesus began, "Not every one that saith unto me, Lord, Lord, shall enter into the Kingdom of Heaven; but he that does the will of my Father which is in Heaven." (Matthew 7:21) A collective gasp swept through the gathering. Here was a distinction, drawn not by mere words or titles, but by actions aligned with the Divine will of the Eternal One.

He continued, unveiling a reality that was both challenging and transformative, "On that day, many will say to me, 'Lord, Lord, did we not prophesy in your name, cast out demons in your name, and perform many miraculous deeds in your name?' And then I will declare to them, 'I never truly knew you: depart from me, you who practice lawlessness and embrace evil.'" (Matthew 7:22-23) The declaration was profound. External acts, no matter how grand, were secondary to the inner alignment with divine truth and righteousness.

As the ripples of his words resonated within each heart, Jesus moved to a powerful parable, grounding his teaching in the familiar. "So, anyone who hears my words and puts them into practice is like a wise person who built their house upon a solid rock" (Matthew 7:24) The audience could almost see this wise builder, painstakingly ensuring that his home, his life, was anchored to an unshakeable foundation.

However, life's tempests were inevitable. "Then the rain poured, the floods surged, and the winds raged against that house, but it did not collapse because its foundation was on solid rock." (Matthew 7:25) In the trials and tribulations, those rooted in divine truth remained unwavering, their spirits untouched by the transient storms of existence.

In contrast, Jesus spoke of another, "But anyone who hears my words and fails to put them into practice is like a foolish person who built their house on shifting sand." (Matthew 7:26) The vulnerability of such a foundation was evident. When adversity struck, "Then the rain poured, the floods surged, and the winds raged against that house, causing it to collapse, and the fall of it was truly great." (Matthew 7:27)

As the echoes of His words faded, a profound realization dawned. The teachings of Jesus were not mere philosophical musings; they were blueprints for life, templates for the soul's journey. The choices made, the foundations chosen, determined not just the course of one's earthly life, but the soul's eternal trajectory.

The impact of His discourse was palpable. "And it came to pass, when Jesus had ended these sayings, the people were astonished at his doctrine: For he taught them as one having authority, and not as the scribes." (Matthew 7:28-29)

In the grand tapestry of existence, Jesus had provided a compass, pointing not to transient worldly gains but to the timeless realm of the I AM. Through parables and teachings, He illuminated pathways to eternity, beckoning every soul to embark on a journey anchored in the unshakeable truth of the Divine.

CHAPTER 8

THE UNVEILING OF DIVINE AUTHORITY

The Dawn of Miracles

After the celestial whispers of wisdom on the mount, Jesus, the Anointed One, embarked on a journey to manifest the Kingdom of God among the mortals. The paths he trod were lit with the gleam of divine promise, as his presence was a balm to the wounded souls. The towns and cities he visited were touched by a breeze of heavenly hope. As he ventured into the realm of earthly adversities, his miracles were a testament to the divine power that the Kingdom of God beheld. Each gesture, each healing touch, each word resonated with the eternal harmony of heaven, giving a glimpse of divine authority to the hearts yearning for salvation.

Emissary of Light:
The Healing Touch of the Divine

The sun hung low in the sky, casting long shadows over the bustling streets and markets. Birds circled overhead, their silhouettes contrasting with the deep blue of the approaching twilight. The wind carried the aroma of freshly baked bread, spices, and the distant sounds of laughter and music from nearby homes. In the midst of this everyday life, a figure stood out. His mere presence seemed to radiate a divine energy, drawing people to Him like moths to a flame.

As Jesus descended from the mountain, having shared profound teachings with those who had ears to hear, a vast crowd eagerly awaited Him, hope etched on every face (Matthew 8:1). Among them was a leper, an outcast, marginalized and shunned by society. His condition, often considered a curse from the gods, kept him separated from loved ones and the community. Yet, in his eyes burned a fire of hope, a desperate yearning.

Kneeling before Jesus, the leper implored, "Lord, if you are willing, you have the power to make me clean." The raw emotion in his voice seemed to pierce the heavens. (Matthew 8:2)

Gazing upon the man with compassion that seemed to emanate from the very core of the universe, Jesus stretched forth His hand, touching him. A gesture so simple, yet so profound in its implications. "I am willing; you are now cleansed," He declared. And in that divine decree, the leprosy was no more. (Matthew 8:3)

News of this miraculous healing spread like wildfire, adding to the tales of wonder surrounding this enigmatic man named Jesus.

However, the journey of miracles was far from over. As Jesus entered Capernaum, a centurion approached Him, desperation evident in his posture and voice. "Lord," he began, "my servant lies at home, afflicted with paralysis, tormented greatly." (Matthew 8:6)

Jesus, ever ready to alleviate suffering, immediately responded, "I will come and heal him." (Matthew 8:7)

But the centurion, a man of great authority yet humbled by his circumstances, replied, "Lord, I am not deserving of your presence within my home, but if you simply speak the word, my servant will be healed. For I am a person under authority, with soldiers under my command. I say to one, 'Go,' and he goes; to another, 'Come,' and he comes; and to my servant, 'Do this,' and he does it." His faith was astounding, recognizing the divine authority of Jesus without having witnessed it firsthand. (Matthew 8:8-9)

Amazed by such unwavering faith, Jesus exclaimed, "Truly I say unto you, I have not found so great faith, no, not in Israel. Many shall come from the east and west, and shall sit down with Abraham, and Isaac, and Jacob, in the Kingdom of Heaven." He continued, foretelling of those who, though they claimed lineage, would find themselves cast out if their hearts weren't true. Then, turning to the centurion, He decreed, "Go on your way, and let it be done to you as you have believed." And in that very hour, the servant was healed, a testament to unwavering faith in the face of adversity. (Matthew 8:10-13)

But the day was far from over. Entering Peter's home, Jesus found Peter's mother-in-law bedridden with a fever. With a gentle touch, He rebuked the ailment, and she arose, restored to full health, serving and attending to their needs. (Matthew 8:14-15)

As evening approached, and shadows grew longer, many were brought to Him, possessed with devils and various infirmities. Fulfilling the prophecy spoken by Isaiah, "Himself took our infirmities, and bore our sicknesses," Jesus cast out the spirits with His word and healed all that were sick. (Matthew 8:16-17)

In the heart of Capernaum, the emissary of light showcased His divine powers, mending broken bodies and spirits, a beacon of hope in a world clouded with despair. With each healing touch and word, He unveiled the boundless love and power of the Eternal One, the great I AM.

Desires of the Heart:
The Cost of True Discipleship

The orange hues of the setting sun painted the heavens, casting a warm glow over the land. The gentle rustling of leaves and the chirping of the crickets created a serene backdrop. But amidst this tranquility, hearts were stirred, souls yearned, and decisions were made.

Word of Jesus' teachings and healings had spread far and wide. Now, not only those in need of healing but also those intrigued by this enigmatic man began to gather. As the crowd swelled, a certain scribe, well-versed in the scriptures, stepped forward. His usual air of confidence slightly trembled with genuine curiosity. "Master," he began with fervor, "I am ready to follow you wherever you lead." (Matthew 8:19)

Jesus, perceiving the depth of his declaration, looked deep into the scribe's eyes. The weight of eternity held in His gaze. "The foxes have holes, and the birds of the air have nests," He began, His voice a

gentle whisper that yet carried an undeniable force, "but the Son of Man has no place to rest His head." (Matthew 8:20)

This wasn't a refusal, but an invitation to understand the profound journey of true discipleship — a path not always laden with comforts or worldly assurances, but one of unwavering commitment.

Another of His disciples, sensing the gravity of the moment, interjected, "Lord, let me first go and bury my father." It was a plea rooted in duty and tradition, a final act of respect to family before embarking on a divine journey. (Matthew 8:21)

Yet, Jesus, ever understanding the urgency of the divine calling and the fleeting nature of worldly commitments, replied, "Follow me; and let the dead bury their dead." (Matthew 8:22)

His response was not one of insensitivity but an invitation to prioritize the spiritual over the temporal. It served as a powerful reminder that the call to follow the path of the Divine, the great I AM, often demands one to transcend societal norms and expectations, focusing instead on the eternal promises that lay ahead.

As twilight gave way to the blanket of night, the crowd reflected upon Jesus' profound words. The cost of discipleship was becoming clearer — it was not merely about being in His presence but about embodying His teachings, making them the cornerstone of one's life, and recognizing the eternal weight of the divine calling.

Whispers of the Tempest: The Unyielding Dominion of His Voice

The horizon was a deep blue, transitioning into the canvas of twilight. With every passing moment, the vast expanse of the sea resonated with the melancholy of impending darkness. The rhythmic dance of the waves, which was once serene, now hinted at the storm that brewed in the distance.

Jesus, with a handful of his disciples, embarked on a journey across the sea. The boat, modest in size, bobbed gently, bearing the weight of destinies that would shape the course of history. The disciples shared hushed conversations, their voices barely rising above the whispers of the wind. But as they sailed further from the shore, the once gentle breeze turned furious, and the murmurs of the sea grew louder.

Suddenly, the tempest unleashed its fury. Massive waves, like the gnarled fingers of a giant, reached out menacingly, threatening to swallow the boat whole.

Panic set in among the disciples. Their faces were painted with fear as they grappled with ropes and sails, desperately trying to keep the boat afloat. Every wave that hit felt like the cold slap of impending doom.

In stark contrast to the chaos, Jesus lay at the stern, enveloped in deep slumber, His trust in the Eternal One unyielding even in the face of nature's wrath.

Frantic, one disciple, his voice almost drowned by the roaring winds, cried out, "Lord, save us! We perish!" (Matthew 8:25)

Jesus slowly opened His eyes, and with a gaze that held both the calm of the abyss and the fire of the cosmos, He rose. "Why are you afraid, you who have such little faith?" He rebuked, his voice piercing through the howl of the storm. Then, turning His attention to the tempest, He commanded, "Peace, be still." (Matthew 8:26)

And just as swiftly as it had started, the storm obeyed. The waves retreated, the winds calmed, and a divine hush enveloped the sea. The disciples, drenched and awestruck, whispered among themselves, "What manner of man is this, that even the winds and the sea obey him?" (Matthew 8:27)

Their journey resumed, but the waters they now navigated held a different story — a testament to the unmatched authority of Jesus' words.

As they reached the other side, in the country of the Gergesenes, they were met with a sight that sent shivers down the spines of even the most hardened among them. Two men, possessed with devils, emerged from the tombs. Their presence was so fearsome that no man dared pass that way. The air grew cold and thick with tension.

Yet, before any of the disciples could react, these tormented souls cried out, "What is our connection to you, Jesus, the Son of God? Have you come here to torment us before the appointed time?" They recognized the divine power He held and feared the judgment He could bring. Sensing a herd of swine grazing

nearby, the devils pleaded, "If you drive us out, allow us to enter into the herd of swine." (Matthew 8:28-31)

With a mere nod, Jesus granted their request. "Go," He commanded. And with that, the possessed men were freed, while the swine, unable to bear the weight of the evil spirits, ran violently down a steep place into the sea and perished. (Matthew 8:32)

The keepers of the swine, their faces pale with a mix of terror and awe, fled to the city, recounting everything they had witnessed — from the deliverance of the possessed men to the demise of the swine. A wave of fear gripped the inhabitants, and they beseeched Jesus to depart from their coasts. (Matthew 8:33-34)

As the chapter closed, the horizon that had once witnessed a raging tempest now bore testament to the unparalleled power and authority of Jesus' words. The very elements of nature and the spiritual realms bowed to His command, reiterating the eternal truth of His dominion over all creation.

Jesus' journey through the earthly realms, manifested divine authority with a tenderness that healed, a word that delivered, and a presence that evoked the awe of heaven. The unfolding of miracles, the unyielding faith of the centurion, and the tempest stilled by his word were but chapters in the eternal story of the Kingdom of God coming to pass amidst the mortal realm.

CHAPTER 9

THE TAPESTRIES OF FAITH AND HEALING

A Trail of Miracles: The Journey Continues

As the dusk of awe from the miracles at Gergesenes settled, the dawn of another day beckoned Jesus to continue His journey. With every step, He unfolded the manifold aspects of the divine realm to the earthly dwellers. The words of His teachings were like soothing balm, His touch a tide of healing, His presence a monument of God's living manifestation among men. The days were not just a measure of time but a chain of divine interventions through Jesus. And as the word spread, the air vibrated with the tales of His miracles, each heart that received His touch became a beacon of faith, shining amid the despair and disease that roamed the lands. The spectacle at Gergesenes was a testament to His authority over the dark realms, a truth that resonated across regions. And as He set sail back to His own city, the seeds of anticipation were sown in every heart that awaited His arrival.

The Weight of Sin: A Paralytic's Liberation

The sun hung low in the sky, casting the city of Capernaum in a golden hue. This bustling city, nestled by the shores of the Sea of Galilee, was a trade hub and an intersection of cultures. Narrow alleys snaked between clay houses, leading to vibrant marketplaces where merchants bartered and fishermen shared tales of the sea.

Amidst the city's din, a hush fell over one home, where a paralytic lay on a bed, his limbs lifeless, his spirit crushed. The room was stifling with the weight of despair and the musky scent of unwashed fabrics. Friends and family gathered around, their voices a mere whisper, the air thick with silent prayers to the I AM.

Suddenly, the murmur of voices outside grew louder, shifting from casual chatter to fervent whispers. "He's here," one voice exclaimed. "The healer, the rabbi, Jesus!"

Not a moment was wasted. Four men, friends of the paralytic, moved with determination. They hoisted the bed, bearing the weight of their immobilized friend, and headed towards where Jesus was teaching. The crowd was immense, and every entrance to the house where Jesus resided was blocked. But love and desperation breed innovation.

Climbing atop the house, they began removing tiles, creating an opening. Dust and debris fell, drawing the attention of those below. As the opening widened, they carefully lowered the bed, bringing their friend directly before Jesus.

The room was thick with anticipation. Jesus, looking up at the hole in the ceiling, then down at the man, saw not just the physical bondage but the deeper chains of sin and guilt. His gaze was filled with compassion as He declared, "Take heart, my child; your sins are forgiven." (Matthew 9:2)

A murmur of disbelief rippled through the crowd. Among them, scribes exchanged uneasy glances, their thoughts echoing loudly, "This man blasphemes! Who can forgive sins but God alone?"

Jesus, discerning their thoughts, confronted them. "Why do you harbor wicked thoughts in your hearts? Which is simpler to say: 'Your sins are forgiven,' or 'Rise up and walk'?" (Matthew 9:4-5)

Then, turning His attention back to the paralytic, He commanded, "Get up, pick up your mat, and go back to your home." (Matthew 9:6) And as the words left His lips, a miracle unfolded. Life surged through the paralytic's limbs, strength replacing weakness. With tears streaming down his face, he stood up, lifted his bed, and began walking, each step a testament to the power of Jesus.

The house erupted in amazement. Those present were seized with both awe and fear, and they glorified the Eternal One, saying, "We have seen strange things today." Their hearts whispered a truth they were only beginning to grasp: In their midst was not just a healer, but one with the authority to forgive sins, a divine echo resonating through the annals of time. (Matthew 9:8)

The Banquet of Redemption: Matthew's New Dawn

From the dwelling that had just witnessed a divine manifestation, Jesus proceeded, his disciples in tow. Capernaum's marketplace was at its bustling peak. Merchants hawked their goods, children darted between stalls, and fishermen shouted the prices of their latest catch. Amid this cacophony stood the tax booth of Matthew, a name synonymous with betrayal in the eyes of his Jewish brethren. As a tax collector for the Romans, he was seen as a traitor, an outcast, enriching himself at the expense of his own people.

Seated on a slightly elevated platform, with ledgers spread out before him, Matthew's eyes scanned the crowd, gauging who owed what. But his stoic facade hid a heart heavy with the weight of isolation and the disdain of his community. In a society where your status and honor were everything, he had neither.

As the sun's rays filtered through the cloth awnings, casting intricate patterns on the ground, an unexpected shadow halted before Matthew's booth. He looked up into the eyes of Jesus, expecting perhaps a word of rebuke or an admonishing glare.

But what he found were eyes filled with an invitation. "Follow me," Jesus said, his voice resonating with an authority that was undeniable and a warmth that was irresistible. (Matthew 9:9)

For a heartbeat, time seemed to pause. The murmurs of the market, the rustle of the leaves, the distant laughter of children - all faded into a hushed silence. Here was the crossroads of Matthew's life. The ledger in his hand, representing his past, and the hand extended to him, beckoning towards a future he had never dared to dream.

With a resolve born out of divine conviction, Matthew rose, leaving behind his booth, his ledgers,

and his old life. He followed Jesus, embarking on a journey from darkness to unparalleled light.

Later, in his own house, Matthew hosted a great feast. Around the table sat a diverse group - tax collectors, sinners, disciples, and Jesus himself. The air was thick with the aroma of grilled fish, fresh bread, and aged wine, but it was also infused with the heady scent of transformation.

But this gathering didn't sit well with everyone. The Pharisees, always on the lookout to criticize Jesus, whispered among themselves, directing their question to the disciples, "Why does your Teacher dine with tax collectors and sinners?" (Matthew 9:11)

Jesus, overhearing, responded, "Those who are in good health do not require a doctor, but those who are sick do." His words, laden with meaning, hung in the air. "Go and understand the significance of this: 'I desire mercy, not sacrifice.' I have not come to summon the righteous, but to call sinners to seek forgiveness and change their ways." (Matthew 9:12-13, referencing Hosea 6:6)

With those words, the heart of Jesus' mission was laid bare. He had come not for the self-proclaimed righteous but for those who acknowledged their brokenness and yearned for redemption. At that banquet table, among the outcasts and the downtrodden, heaven's love was on full display, heralding the dawn of a new era.

The Tapestry of Renewal: Old Forms, New Wine

In the wake of the banquet, with its joyous atmosphere still lingering in the air, a group approached Jesus. Among them were the disciples of John the Baptist, a figure revered for his asceticism and unwavering dedication to the preparation of the Messiah's coming.

With genuine curiosity and perhaps a touch of reproach, they inquired, "Why do we and the Pharisees fast often, but thy disciples fast not?" (Matthew 9:14) Their question was not just about the act of fasting,

but the underlying spiritual discipline and commitment it represented. Why, they wondered, did Jesus' followers not subject themselves to the same rigorous spiritual exercises?

Jesus, ever patient, drew them in with a parable that spoke to the heart of the matter. "Can the friends of the bridegroom grieve while he is in their presence? But the time will come when the bridegroom will be taken away from them, and then they will fast." (Matthew 9:15)

His words painted a vivid picture. Imagine a wedding celebration, full of joy, music, and dancing. Would it be fitting for the groom's friends to mourn in the midst of such festivity? The very idea was preposterous. The presence of the groom - or, in this case, the Messiah - was a time for celebration, not mourning.

But Jesus did not stop there. He expanded his teaching, drawing from the familiar to explain the unfamiliar. "No one attaches a new piece of cloth to an old garment, for the new patch will shrink and worsen the tear in the old fabric." (Matthew 9:16)

His listeners, many of whom wore garments patched multiple times, understood immediately. A new piece of cloth would shrink after its first wash, pulling away from the old fabric and worsening the tear.

Likewise, Jesus continued, "No one pours new wine into old bottles, or else the bottles will break, the wine will spill, and both will be lost. Instead, they pour new wine into new bottles, preserving both." (Matthew 9:17)

The message was profound in its clarity. The new teachings and new covenant Jesus brought couldn't be confined within the old structures and traditions. New wine required new wineskins, and the transformative power of Jesus' message required new forms and practices.

His teachings weren't in opposition to the old; rather, they were its fulfillment, an evolution, a new chapter in the eternal relationship between God and man. The listeners were left with an understanding that while traditions have their place, the movement of the Spirit was dynamic, evolving, and ever new.

Whispers of Faith:
The Veil Between Hope and Miracles

As the day's lessons continued to unfold, an air of urgency interrupted the gathering. A certain ruler, whose stature in society was evident by the ornate

robes he wore, approached Jesus, his eyes reddened from tears and desperation evident in every step. Kneeling before the Master, he implored, "My daughter has just passed away, but if you come and place your hand upon her, she will be restored to life." (Matthew 9:18)

The plea hung heavily in the air. Here was a man, used to command and authority, humbling himself in the face of overwhelming grief and helplessness. But underlying his desperation was a remarkable belief—a belief in Jesus' power over even death.

As Jesus and His disciples began to move in response, they encountered a scene familiar to the bustling streets of that age. Amid the throngs of people, a woman, frail and worn from twelve long years of ailment, moved stealthily. She had heard of Jesus, of the miracles He performed, and the power in His words. This hearing had kindled a flame of faith within her. "If only I can touch His robe," she whispered to herself, driven by a hope that had been kindled from tales of His deeds, "I will be healed." (Matthew 9:21)

In a world defined by tangible proofs, her belief was grounded in something she had yet to see but had only heard. Such is the nature of faith—it springs from hearing, and hearing by the word of God. Drawing from this well of faith, she reached out and touched the hem of His garment.

Suddenly, Jesus stopped, turning to look at her. His gaze was not one of rebuke but of understanding and compassion. "Daughter," He began, His voice filled with tenderness and joy, "take heart; your faith has brought about your complete healing." (Matthew 9:22) In that instant, her ailment vanished, and she stood transformed, not just in body but in spirit.

The journey resumed, and soon Jesus was at the ruler's house. The scene was one of mourning. Wailers filled the air with their cries, a grim testament to the finality of death. But with an authority echoing the Eternal One, Jesus declared, "Please step aside, for the young girl is not deceased; she is merely sleeping." (Matthew 9:24) His words were met with mocking laughter from the crowd, unable to comprehend the depth of His authority.

Yet, undeterred, He entered the room where the young girl lay, taking her by the hand. In that sacred moment, where hope met the impossible, she arose, a living testimony to the faith of her father and the unmatched power of Jesus.

These intertwined tales of faith, from a ruler and a woman seemingly worlds apart, bore testament to a singular truth: Faith, no matter its origin, when placed in the One with true authority, can move the very mountains of despair, illness, and even death.

Echoes of Restoration:
The All-Encompassing Embrace of Healing

As Jesus journeyed further, two blind men began trailing Him, their keen ears attuned to His footsteps. The whispers around them, stories of the miracles He had performed, acted as a guiding star to their faith. With voices tinged with hope, they cried out, "You, Son of David, show us your mercy!" (Matthew 9:27)

Upon entering a dwelling, these men, driven by their undying belief, followed Him. Their world was shrouded in darkness, but their spirits glimpsed a dawn of hope in Jesus. Turning to them, Jesus probed the depths of their hearts with a question that wasn't for His benefit, but theirs: "Do you truly believe that I have the power to accomplish this?" It was an invitation, an opening for them to vocalize their faith. With fervor, they responded, "Yea, Lord." (Matthew 9:28)

Their affirmation was more than mere words. It was a declaration of trust, a testament to countless tales of healing they had heard. Touched by their unwavering belief, Jesus, with hands that had shaped galaxies, gently touched their eyes. "Let it be done to you as your faith believes." He declared. (Matthew 9:29) The veil of darkness that had long bound them was lifted, revealing a world awash with light and color.

But the tales of wonder did not end there. As the once-blind men stepped out, their eyes gleaming with gratitude and wonder, another was brought forth. A man, demon-possessed and mute, stood as a silent testament to the spiritual battles that raged unseen. With a mere word of authority, Jesus cast out the foul spirit. And the man, his voice restored, spoke—his every word a hymn of praise and testament to the Savior's power. (Matthew 9:32-33)

The multitudes marveled, saying, "Such a thing has never been witnessed in Israel before." (Matthew 9:33) Yet, among them, the Pharisees whispered with skepticism, "He expels demons by the ruler of demons." (Matthew 9:34) Even amidst undeniable evidence of divine power, the hearts of some remained shrouded in doubt.

Yet, for all who approached Him, for all who believed, no ailment was too great, no chain too strong. From whispered tales of hope to visible transformations, Jesus' authority and power knew no bounds. In His presence, the blind saw, the mute spoke, and the oppressed found freedom. Every touch, every word from Him brought forth healing—not just of the body but of the soul.

The Fields Ripe for Harvest

As Jesus traversed the regions of Judea and the surrounding cities, He carried with Him not just the power of miracles, but an observant eye that pierced through the façades of society. Wherever His gaze landed, He saw humanity in its rawest form—burdened, weary, and teetering on the precipice of despair. Each village, every city was like an open wound, revealing the desperate needs of its people. They were scattered, like sheep having no shepherd—lost, leaderless, and longing. (Matthew 9:36)

Amidst the grandeur of temples and the bustling markets, amidst the cries of merchants and the laughter of children, a deeper, silent cry echoed—a cry of souls yearning for solace, for salvation. It was this silent cry, this unseen torment that stirred the depths of Jesus' compassionate heart.

One evening, as the sun painted the horizon in hues of gold and crimson, Jesus gathered His disciples around a campfire. The flickering flames illuminated their faces, casting shadows that danced with the night. Drawing their attention to the vast fields around them, now bathed in twilight, Jesus spoke, "The harvest truly is plenteous, but the laborers are few." (Matthew 9:37) The fields, seemingly serene, held a deeper symbolism—a world waiting, yearning for hope and restoration.

He then breathed a directive, one that hinted at their grand mission ahead, "So, pray to the Lord of the harvest, asking Him to send workers into His fields." (Matthew 9:38) It wasn't merely a call to observe, but an invitation to partake, to join the divine mission of soul-harvesting.

The disciples listened, the weight of the task ahead slowly dawning upon them. They were to be the bearers of light, the harbingers of hope. Jesus, in His divine foresight, was preparing them. They weren't just to be spectators of miracles; they were to be the instruments of change in a world desperately seeking salvation.

And as the fire dwindled, and the night wrapped them in its embrace, the disciples sat in contemplative silence, their hearts ignited with purpose, ready to answer the call of the harvest.

As the dusk settled, the tales of the day echoed through the hearts across regions. The words of Jesus, His miracles, were not mere events but a spectrum of divine interventions, illustrating the unfathomable dimensions of God's kingdom. And as the night sky veiled the earthly, the stars twinkled with the glory of the divine, illuminating the hearts with a promise of a new dawn, a dawn of hope, faith, and divine love.

Chapter 10

The Transference of the Heavenly Mantle

A Dawning Epoch: The Mantle Awaits its Bearers

The glorious sun casting its first rays onto the ancient land of Judea symbolized a dawn of new hope, faith, and divine intervention. The rhythmic chirping of birds, a melody to the ears, resonated through the bustling city of Capernaum, creating a harmonious hymn with the gentle rustling of olive trees. Amidst the serene morning, the city was stirring with whispers about the wandering healer, Jesus of Nazareth, who, in the eyes of believers, was the Anointed One, and in the hearts of the afflicted, a fountain of divine grace.

As the curtain of night lifted, the day unfolded a new chapter in the divine epic that was transpiring in the earthly realm. The gospel of the Kingdom of God was like an ever-spreading sacred fire, kindling the hearts of the seeking, mending the broken, and challenging the rigid orthodoxy of religious leaders. The echoes of Jesus' teachings from the Sermon on the Mount still vibrated through the hearts across regions, and the deeds of mercy that followed were like a soothing balm on the wounds of the weary.

Anointing the Chosen Twelve

In the hours that followed their contemplative night under the stars, a renewed vigor emanated from the disciples. They sensed an impending call, a mission that would transform their lives forever. The horizon had barely begun to show the first golden hues when Jesus, His face illuminated by the rising sun, stood atop a small hillock, beckoning His followers.

Drawing them close, He began to name them, not just as followers, but as emissaries—apostles chosen to herald the dawn of a new era. "Simon, also known as Peter, and his brother Andrew; James, son of Zebedee, and his brother John; Philip and Bartholomew; Thomas and Matthew the tax collector; James, son of Alphaeus, and Thaddaeus; Simon the Zealot, and Judas Iscariot." (Matthew 10:2-4)

With the election complete, Jesus, His gaze piercing into their souls, endowed them with powers that were till then exclusive to Him. "I give unto you power against unclean spirits, to cast them out, and to heal all manner of sickness and all manner of disease." (Matthew 10:1)

The air was thick with anticipation as Jesus, emphasizing the weight of their mission, said, "Do not journey into the lands of the Gentiles, and do not enter any city of the Samaritans. Instead, go to the lost sheep of the house of Israel. As you go, proclaim, 'The Kingdom of Heaven is near.'" (Matthew 10:5-7)

Guidance for the Journey Ahead

Heeding the interconnectedness of their last discussion about the ripe harvest, Jesus continued, "Heal the sick, purify the lepers, bring the dead back to life, and cast out demons. You have received freely, so give freely" Their mission was clear—they were to be the hands of Jesus, bringing relief, restoration, and revival. (Matthew 10:8)

For generations, humanity had been bound in the suffocating grasp of Satan. Chains of despair, sickness, and spiritual blindness had been the plight of many. Towns and villages lived under a shadow, a world where true freedom seemed like a distant dream. The dark prince reveled in the anguish of souls, delighting in the chaos he wrought, watching as hope ebbed away from the hearts of men and women.

But in this pivotal moment in history, Jesus, the Light of the World, was piercing through this profound darkness. He came as the beacon of hope, the embodiment of the I AM, determined to shatter the chains, to free those ensnared, and to restore sight to the blinded eyes. His mission was to declare that the reign of darkness was coming to an end, and the dawn of the Kingdom of Heaven was breaking.

In a gentle yet firm tone, Jesus provided them practical counsel for their journey, "Do not carry gold, silver, or brass in your purses, nor a bag for your journey, nor two coats, nor shoes, nor staffs. The laborer deserves their sustenance." (Matthew 10:9-10)

As they journeyed, they would find both acceptance and rejection. To those who welcomed them, they were to let their peace come upon that house. Yet, to those that resisted, they were to shake off the very dust from their feet as they departed, a symbolic act of judgment and a testament to the consequences of refusing the message of the Kingdom. (Matthew 10:11-15)

With these words, Jesus was not just sending them on a mission; He was embarking them on an epic journey of faith, trust, and divine encounters—a journey where they would be the bearers of the Eternal Dawn, pushing back the shadows of despair and lighting up the world with the luminous message of the Kingdom of Heaven.

Facing the Shadows: The Price of Defiance

Their journey wouldn't merely be one of miracles and jubilant praises. As the bearers of the Eternal Dawn, the disciples would also have to face the men-

acing shadows that sought to extinguish this emerging light. Jesus, with a gaze that seemed to pierce the very fabric of time, spoke words of caution and preparation, "See, I am sending you out like sheep among wolves. Therefore, be as wise as serpents and as innocent as doves." (Matthew 10:16)

As the disciples listened intently, they could sense the weight and gravity of the mission that lay before them. It was a task that demanded more than just passion; it required discernment, wisdom, and a heart rooted deeply in the Eternal One. "Beware of men," Jesus continued, "for they will deliver you up to the councils, and they will scourge you in their synagogues." (Matthew 10:17) The message they carried, though filled with hope and light, was also a direct challenge to the existing powers, both seen and unseen.

The disciples were not to be deterred by these threats. Jesus assured them that when confronted, the Spirit of the Eternal One would give them the words, a divine eloquence that no opponent could resist or refute. "But when they deliver you up, take no thought how or what you will speak: for it will be given to you in that same hour what you will speak. For it is not you that speak, but the Spirit of your Father which speaks in you." (Matthew 10:19-20)

The road to ushering in the Kingdom was fraught with trials and trepidations. Jesus painted a picture of a world that would be turned upside down by their message—a world where families would be divided because of the name of Christ. "And you will be hated of all men for my name's sake: but he that endures to the end will be saved." (Matthew 10:22)

Yet, even in the face of such stark realities, there was a glimmer of hope. "When they persecute you in one city, move on to another to continue your mission." Jesus instructed, emphasizing the importance of resilience and adaptability in their divine mission. (Matthew 10:23)

Drawing a profound parallel, Jesus reminded them, "A disciple is not superior to their master, nor is a servant greater than their lord. It suffices for the disciple to be like their master and the servant like their lord. If they have accused the master of the house of being Beelzebub, how much more will they slander those of his household?" (Matthew 10:24-25) Just as Jesus, the beacon of hope and light, faced opposition, so too would His followers. They were stepping into a world where the forces of darkness would retaliate, but they would do so armed with the power and protection of the I AM, pushing back against the shad-

ows with the blazing glory of the Kingdom of Heaven.

Echoes in the Silence:
Undying Truths Amidst the Shadows

From the somber note of trials and persecutions, Jesus pivoted, casting a gaze of unyielding determination upon His disciples. "Do not be afraid," He began, igniting the embers of courage within their souls, "for there is nothing concealed that will not be unveiled, and nothing hidden that will not be made known." (Matthew 10:26)

As they stood there, absorbing the gravity of their mission and the challenges it would pose, the Savior's voice resonated with unwavering authority, echoing across the vast landscapes of history and time. "What I share with you in the shadows, proclaim openly in the light, and what you hear whispered, declare from the housetops." (Matthew 10:27) Their task was not merely to bear witness to the truth but to amplify it, to let the whispers of heaven resound like thunder across the earth.

While the path was fraught with danger, Jesus reminded them of the grander perspective. "And fear not them which kill the body, but are not able to kill

the soul: but rather fear Him which is able to destroy both soul and body in hell." (Matthew 10:28) The threats they faced, though real, were ephemeral compared to the eternal truths they bore.

He continued with a tender metaphor, "Aren't two sparrows sold for a small coin? Yet not one of them falls to the ground without your Father's knowledge. Even the number of hairs on your head is meticulously counted by Him." (Matthew 10:29-30) The disciples, amidst the vast cosmos, were intimately known and cared for by the Eternal One. Each of them held a unique, irreplaceable place in the grand tapestry of creation.

Jesus presented a challenge, one that resonated with the depth of their beings, "Therefore, whoever openly acknowledges me before others, I will also acknowledge before my Father in heaven. But those who deny me before others, I will also deny before my Father in heaven." (Matthew 10:32-33) The call was clear: boldness in proclamation, unwavering allegiance to the truth.

Swords of Division:
The Cost of Allegiance

The path of the disciples was not one solely of tranquility and acceptance. It was a path marked by the deep divisions that truth inevitably brings when it clashes with the established order. "Do not think that I have come to bring peace to the earth. I have not come to bring peace, but a sword," Jesus declared, foretelling the discord that His message would introduce, even among the closest of kin. (Matthew 10:34)

This 'sword'—a metaphor for the division—spoke of the separation between those who would accept His message and those who would reject it. A division so profound, it would pierce the familial bonds that had, until then, seemed unbreakable. "For I have come to set a man against his father, and a daughter against her mother, and a daughter-in-law against her mother-in-law," He continued, illustrating the inevitable choice that would confront every person who heard His call. (Matthew 10:35)

His words, stark and uncompromising, echoed with a sobering truth: "And a person's enemies will be those of his own household." (Matthew 10:36) It was a pronouncement that loyalty to the Gospel could exact a high personal toll, demanding allegiance that transcended even the most fundamental human relationships.

The gravity of discipleship's demand was clear, as Jesus explained, "Whoever loves father or mother more than me is not worthy of me, and whoever loves son or daughter more than me is not worthy of me." (Matthew 10:37) Love for family, while sacred, was not to supersede the love for Him and His mission. This was the essence of the Gospel—a radical call to prioritize the eternal over the temporal, the divine over the familial.

"And whoever does not take his cross and follow me is not worthy of me," Jesus concluded. (Matthew 10:38) The 'cross'—an instrument of death and a symbol of ultimate sacrifice—was now to be their emblem of commitment, an outward sign of their inward dedication to the path He had set before them.

"Whoever finds his life will lose it, and whoever loses his life for my sake will find it," He promised. (Matthew 10:39) In these paradoxical words lay the heart of the Gospel's mystery—that in the very act of surrendering to Christ, one would discover true life, a life unshackled from the world's transient nature and aligned with the eternal purpose of the I AM.

With these solemn words, Jesus prepared His followers for the journey ahead, one that would challenge them to the core, but also one that would lead them to the fulfillment found only in His presence.

The Reward of the Righteous

Jesus then painted a picture of the reciprocal blessings of the Kingdom, "He that receives you receives me, and he that receives me receives him that sent me." (Matthew 10:40) In receiving the disciples, one was not merely welcoming weary travelers but was inviting in the very presence of Jesus and, by extension, the Eternal One who had commissioned Him. This was a profound unity of purpose and identity, where the lines between the sender and the sent were divinely blurred.

To underscore this solidarity, Jesus offered reassurance of reward not just for the grand acts of sacrifice, but also for the smallest gestures of kindness, "And whosoever shall give to drink unto one of these little ones a cup of cold water only in the name of a disciple, verily I say unto you, he shall in no wise lose his reward." (Matthew 10:42) Here, Jesus affirmed the Kingdom's values—where the giving of a cup of water, an act so humble and so simple, was seen and cherished by the Eternal One.

As they dispersed, each step they took was a step into the epic adventure that awaited. The words of Jesus were like a divine map engraved in their hearts, leading them through the labyrinth of earthly existence towards the manifestation of the Kingdom of Heaven.

The world they stepped into was the same, yet their eyes were now opened to the unseen, their ears attuned to the divine harmonies, and their hearts pulsated with the rhythm of heavenly purposes.

Thus commenced the saga of the twelve, chosen to disrupt the kingdom of darkness, chosen to illuminate the earthly with the heavenly, chosen to be the living epistles of the narrative of the I AM.

CHAPTER 11

THE VOICE OF THE ANCIENT ECHO

Unveiling the Shrouded Whisper

As dawn's first light grazes the historic landscape of Machaerus, the world seems to pulse with an energy, both old and new. The stories whispered through these ancient stones are about to intertwine with the urgent quests of faithful disciples, the illuminating teachings of Jesus, and the undeniable signs of a prophecy nearing fulfillment. While John the Baptist's spirit remains unshackled despite his chains, a broader narrative is taking shape. The age-old dance between divine revelations and human skepticism, salvation's beckoning and hearts yearning for truth, is once again unfolding.

Messengers in the Midst of Uncertainty

The sun rose over the sprawling city of Machaerus, casting its golden rays over the ancient stones and echoing the promises of a new day. Within the confines of this fortress, imprisoned by Herod, was John the Baptist. Though held captive by chains, his spirit remained unshackled, ever vigilant for signs of the coming Messiah. Hearing of Jesus' deeds, he sent forth two of his closest disciples on an urgent quest to seek answers. (Matthew 11:1-2)

As they weaved through bustling marketplaces and dusty roads, the sounds of merchants peddling their wares, children playing, and the hum of daily life were all around. Yet, their focus was singular - they had to find Jesus. When they finally stood before Him, their expressions were a mix of awe and uncertainty. With a deep breath, one voiced their burning question, "Are you the one who was foretold to come, or should we anticipate another?" (Matthew 11:3)

Jesus, ever the patient teacher, didn't offer a simple answer. Instead, He beckoned them to observe. "Go and show John again those things which you do hear and see: The blind receive their sight, and the lame walk, the lepers are cleansed, and the deaf hear, the dead are raised up, and the poor have the gospel preached to them." (Matthew 11:4-5) The miracles around them were not just acts of kindness; they were the fulfillment of prophecies, tangible proofs of divine power.

As John's disciples departed, their hearts abuzz with newfound revelations, Jesus addressed the multitudes about the wilderness prophet. "Why did you journey into the wilderness? To witness a reed swaying in the wind? Or did you venture out to see a man dressed in luxurious garments? Those who wear such clothing reside in the houses of kings. But what was your purpose in going? To witness a prophet? Yes, I tell you, and even more than a prophet." (Matthew 11:7-9) His words painted John not as a mere herald but as the pivotal figure Isaiah once spoke of, the preparer of the Lord's path. (Matthew 11:10)

Yet, even amidst these affirmations, Jesus recognized the divisive nature of their missions. "John came, refraining from both eating and drinking, and they accused him of being possessed by a demon. The Son of Man, on the other hand, came partaking in food and drink, and they labeled Him as a glutton and a wine-drinker, a friend of tax collectors and sinners." (Matthew 11:18-19) The world often misunderstands those sent by the Eternal One, but wisdom would be justified by her children.

In the backdrop of skepticism, Jesus' mission continued unabated. The Kingdom's message was clear, and those with ears attuned to the eternal resonances would hear it. The stage was set for the revelation of deeper truths and the call to a world yearning for salvation. The narrative of redemption was unfolding, and all were beckoned to partake in its grandeur.

The Fire of Unrepentance

The sun glinted off the ancient stones of the cities as Jesus moved among them, his message echoing through their streets. These were places that had witnessed His most profound miracles, where the blind were made to see and the lame to dance. But even after such divine acts, the hearts of many remained hardened.

In Chorazin, the city nestled amidst fertile plains, children played on streets where the blind once regained their sight. In Bethsaida, near the shores of the sparkling Sea of Galilee, fishermen cast their nets, possibly overlooking the very waters where miraculous catches had been hauled. And yet, in these very cities, a shroud of spiritual darkness lingered.

It was not merely disappointment in His voice; it was a deep, resonant fury. "Woe unto thee, Chorazin! woe unto thee, Bethsaida! For if the mighty works, which were done in you, had been done in Tyre and Sidon, they would have repented long ago in sackcloth and ashes," Jesus proclaimed. His voice rose with the intensity of His message, echoing across the landscape. The very ground seemed to tremble under the weight of His words. (Matthew 11:21)

Even the fabled cities of Tyre and Sidon, with their storied past and sinful reputations, would have turned from their wicked ways had they witnessed such miracles. This comparison amplified the gravity of the unrepentance of Chorazin and Bethsaida.

But He did not stop there. Capernaum, the bustling fishing hub, the city that had been elevated to the heavens with miracles and teachings, would face a stark fate. "And as for you, Capernaum," Jesus continued with profound intensity, "who has been raised to the heights of heaven, you will be cast down to the depths of hell. If the remarkable deeds performed in your midst had occurred in Sodom, it would have endured to this very day." The ancient city of Sodom, known for its wickedness and subsequent divine judgment, stood as a stark backdrop to His words. Capernaum's failure to repent was even more grievous in light of the abundant grace it had received. (Matthew 11:23)

It was a haunting image—these thriving cities, juxtaposed with those of old that had faced the wrath of the Eternal One. The people in these cities had witnessed firsthand the power of the I AM, and yet, their hearts were unmoved.

Yet, even in His rebuke, there was a hint of the boundless love and mercy of Jesus. It was a call—a desperate, passionate plea—for them to recognize the weight of their choices, to turn from their paths of destruction and embrace the saving grace He offered. The following moments would reveal an invitation, an open hand amidst the storm of rebuke. But for now, the weight of their decisions hung heavily in the air.

The Revealed Mystery of the Eternal One

As the weight of Jesus's rebuke settled over the cities, a serene stillness draped the landscape. But amidst that silence, a murmur of confusion persisted.

The learned men of the age, the scholars and philosophers, had struggled to grasp the true essence of Jesus's teachings. They poured over scriptures, debated in hushed tones in synagogues, yet the Kingdom of God eluded their understanding.

Jesus, sensing the depth of this mystery and the hearts of those who sought truth, began to speak. His voice, gentle yet filled with authority, broke the silence, "I express my gratitude to you, O Father, the Sovereign of heaven and earth, for concealing these truths from the wise and learned, and unveiling them to those who are innocent and humble." (Matthew 11:25)

It was a paradoxical truth: while the learned sought God in complexity and debate, the simple, child-like hearts received Him with unassuming faith. Theirs was not a faith burdened by layers of human wisdom but was pure and trusting. In their innocence, they perceived the profound truths that evaded the most scholarly.

Continuing, Jesus unveiled one of the deepest mysteries of the cosmos, "All things have been entrusted to me by my Father, and no one truly comprehends the Son except the Father, just as no one truly understands the Father except the Son, and those to

whom the Son graciously chooses to reveal Him." (Matthew 11:27)

The profundity of this declaration was breathtaking. In Jesus's human nature, He was the Son—visible, tangible, and perceivable by the senses. Yet, in His divinity, He was one with the Father—the Eternal One, the I AM. This wasn't merely about titles or designations; it was about essence and being. To truly know the Son in His entirety was to understand His divine nature, a revelation only possible by the Father. And to recognize the Father, one must see and accept the Son, for He was the embodiment, the perfect reflection of the Father's heart.

This divine interconnectedness, this unbreakable bond between the Son and the Father, was foundational. One couldn't claim to know the Father without embracing the Son who stood before them, and to know the Son spiritually, one had to cultivate an intimate relationship with the Father, who is Spirit. This was not mere theology; it was the doorway to salvation and eternal communion.

But Jesus's message wasn't just a theological exposition. It was an invitation—a call echoing through time and space. "Come to me, all of you who toil and carry heavy burdens, and I will grant you peace. Ac-

cept my yoke and learn from me, for I am gentle and humble in heart, and you will discover tranquility for your souls. My yoke is manageable, and my load is light." (Matthew 11:28-30)

For those who understood, for those wearied by the struggles of life and the burdens of sin, Jesus offered solace. In Him was rest, peace, and eternal communion with the Father. This was the essence of the Kingdom—a realm not just of rules but of relationship, of knowing and being known by the I AM.

As the sun began its descent, casting long shadows across the land, Jesus's words lingered in the air. The mysteries He revealed weren't for mere debate or philosophical discourse; they were life-altering truths. His teachings were an invitation to step into the boundless realm of God's love, a kingdom beyond human comprehension yet accessible through faith. Those with ears to hear and hearts to understand would embark on an epic journey, one that would lead them to the very heart of the I AM.

CHAPTER 12

THE PHARISEES' VEILED DILEMMA

The Dawning Veil of Truth

Following the profound echoes of divine wisdom that resonated through the plains of Galilee, the dawn witnessed a changing tide in Jesus' mission. The celestial invitation for eternal rest had left the masses in ponderous silence. However, a brooding storm brewed in the hearts of the Pharisees who saw the divine illumination as a threat to their earthly dominions. The veiled enmity was gradually moving towards an inevitable confrontation, setting the stage for a clash between the earthly and the divine.

As the first rays of the sun cast a gentle glow upon the earth, the day ahead held promises of unveiling truths that had long been shrouded in the shadows of ritualistic practices. Jesus and His disciples, filled with a resolve as steady as the rising sun, set forth towards the fields, ready to spread the beams of divine insight into the rigid interpretations of law that held many in bondage.

The Fields of Providence

In the sun-baked lands of Judea, fields of golden wheat danced in harmony with the wind. These fields, under the ancient law, held an extraordinary purpose. By divine mandate, landowners were instructed to leave a portion of their cultivation untouched, allowing the less fortunate, the travel-

ers, and the poor to glean from it and find sustenance (Leviticus 19:9-10). It was a practice that embodied God's unyielding compassion for His children, ensuring that none would go hungry in the land He had blessed.

On one such Sabbath day, as the city of Jerusalem basked under the mild warmth of the sun, Jesus and His disciples ambled through these very fields. Hungry from their journey, they began to pluck ears of grain, rubbing them in their hands to separate the kernels from the chaff. It was a simple act, yet one that would set the stage for a profound revelation. (Matthew 12:1)

From a distance, the ever-watchful eyes of the Pharisees observed them. These religious leaders, having wrapped themselves in layers of man-made traditions and rules, had often distorted God's original intent for the law. They saw this act of plucking grain on the Sabbath as a violation, even though the true law of God never imposed such a restriction. It was a reflection of how the Pharisees had often added to God's pure laws with their own interpretations. (Matthew 12:2)

Upon seeing their disapproving glares, Jesus, in His typical manner, did not offer a direct rebuttal. Instead, He delved into the annals of their revered scriptures, bringing forth a tale from the past. "Have you not read," Jesus began, invoking the story of David when he and his men were famished. David had entered the house of God and eaten the consecrated bread, which was not lawful for him to consume but only for the priests. Yet, God did not condemn David. (1 Samuel 21:1-6; Matthew 12:3-4)

Furthermore, Jesus shed light on another nuance of the law, "Or have you not read in the Law, how that on the Sabbath days the priests in the temple profane the Sabbath, and are blameless?" He referenced the priests who work in the temple on the Sabbath, performing sacrifices and other duties, and yet they remain guiltless. (Numbers 28:9-10; Matthew 12:5)

Then, with a gravity that silenced the murmurs around Him, Jesus made a declaration that shook the very foundation of their beliefs, "But I say unto you, That in this place is one greater than the temple." (Matthew 12:6) The temple, the epicenter of their faith, the dwelling place of the Most High, was revered above all. Yet, here stood Jesus, claiming His authority and essence surpassed even that of this magnificent edifice. It was a testament not just to His divine nature but to the profound shift that was taking place in the spiritual realm.

Further emphasizing His authority, He added, "For the Son of Man is Lord even of the Sabbath day." (Matthew 12:8) The Sabbath, a day set aside by the Eternal One, the I AM, was under the dominion of Jesus. In proclaiming this, Jesus was not merely asserting His authority over a day but highlighting His intricate connection and unity with the Father. It was a proclamation of His divinity and His role in the grand cosmic narrative.

In these fields, amidst the golden grain, Jesus dismantled man-made traditions that had veiled the true essence of the Sabbath. It wasn't just about rules and rituals; it was about mercy, compassion, and recognizing the Lord of the Sabbath. As the winds whispered through the fields, the dance of wheat and grain seemed to echo the very rhythm of this revelation, a blend of authority and mercy, beckoning all to see the heart of the Eternal One. (Matthew 12:1-8)

The Synagogue's Dilemma

The alleys of the city led Jesus and His disciples to one of the synagogues—a place of learning, debate, and spiritual nourishment. Its grand stone architecture, layered with history and reverence, stood majestically under the azure sky. Inside, the soft hum of prayer and contemplation resonated, but it was about to be disrupted by a poignant demonstration of divine compassion.

Within the confines of the synagogue was a man with a withered hand. The muscles had long atrophied, and the skin was drawn tight over bone. The man's hand hung limp at his side, a constant reminder of his ailment. Seeing him, the Pharisees, ever eager to find fault in Jesus, posed a loaded question: "Is it lawful to heal on the Sabbath days?" They hoped to trap Jesus in a contradiction, leveraging their man-made interpretations of the Sabbath against Him. (Matthew 12:10)

Drawing everyone's attention to the man, Jesus responded not with a direct answer but with a poignant question of His own, "What man among you, having a sheep that falls into a pit on the Sabbath, will not lay hold on it and lift it out?" He illustrated that even in their own practices, the Pharisees showed more compassion to an animal than to a fellow man, showcasing the hypocrisy of their man-made laws. It was clear: doing good was never prohibited on the Sabbath. (Matthew 12:11)

Gazing deeply into the eyes of the afflicted man, Jesus declared, "It is lawful to do well on the Sabbath days." With a voice filled with divine authority and compassion, He then commanded, "Extend your hand." The man, with faith sparkling in his eyes, obeyed—and his hand was miraculously restored, as whole as the other. The entire synagogue reverberated with the energy of the miracle, a profound testament to God's power and mercy. (Matthew 12:12-13)

Yet, in the midst of this divine display, the Pharisees' hearts hardened. The very essence of the Sabbath was being unveiled before them, but they were blinded by their rigid adherence to their traditions. They perceived Jesus as a threat, not only to their authority but also to the intricate web of rules and regulations they had spun around the law. In the shadows of the synagogue, whispers of retaliation began to stir, revealing the sinister intentions brewing in their hearts against Jesus. (Matthew 12:14)

It's crucial to reflect on Jesus' earlier words, "I desire compassion, not ritual sacrifice" (Matthew 12:7). This quote, drawn from the prophet Hosea (Hosea 6:6), underscores God's desire for genuine compassion and love over mere ritualistic practices. The Eternal One always prioritized the well-being of His children over rigid adherence to ceremonies. Jesus emphasized this, revealing that the heart of God's law was always centered on mercy, love, and compassion, rather than empty sacrifices and rituals.

Whispers of Revolution

Jesus, with His divine foresight, knew the Pharisees's clandestine schemes. Quietly, without drawing attention, He withdrew from Jerusalem. His exit wasn't out of fear, but out of divine timing; His purpose wasn't yet fulfilled. Those who followed Him were many—men, women, and children—each bearing their tales of pain, suffering, and hope. To them, He was the embodiment of divine promise, and He continued to heal them all. But He instructed them not to reveal His whereabouts. The Messiah operated not with an ostentatious display but with humble, measured steps, always in sync with the divine plan (Matthew 12:15-16).

The narrative of Jesus' journey was reminiscent of the ancient prophecies. The words of the prophet Isaiah rang true, echoing through the annals of time: "Here is my chosen servant, my beloved, in whom my soul delights. I will bestow my Spirit upon him, and he will bring justice to the Gentiles. He will not quarrel or raise his voice in the streets. A bruised reed he will not break, and a smoldering wick he will not extinguish, until he brings forth justice to victory. The Gentiles will place their trust in his name." (Matthew 12:18-21, referencing Isaiah 42:1-4).

The prophecy depicted a Savior who was gentle yet powerful, a leader who would not crush the weak but restore them, a beacon of hope not just for Israel but for all nations. In Jesus, this vision was incarnate—His every action and decision molded by an unwavering commitment to the greater good and the

grand divine tapestry. His destiny was clear, and even in the midst of adversities, He continued His mission, ensuring that hope would shine even in the darkest corners of the earth.

Duality of Power:
Light and Shadow

The city was a haven of whispers and tales, where miracles and wonders were recounted like legends of old. And on this day, another story emerged from the midst—of a man, once blind and mute, both his vision and voice restored in an astonishing act of healing. The murmurs grew louder, the throngs amassing around Jesus, admiration in their eyes. They questioned, "Could this be the Son of David?" hinting at the age-old prophecy of the promised Messiah, the one to come from David's lineage. (Matthew 12:22-23)

But in the midst of this sea of believers, the Pharisees stood as jagged rocks, steadfast in their disbelief. Their hearts, hardened by jealousy and the thirst for power, sought an explanation that would undermine Jesus. "This man does not cast out demons except by Beelzebub, the ruler of demons," they proclaimed. By suggesting that Jesus was in league with the devil, they aimed to dissuade the masses from seeing Him as the

Messiah, lest His influence outgrow theirs. (Matthew 12:24)

Jesus, discerning their thoughts, addressed them with a poignant parable. "Every kingdom divided against itself is brought to desolation. How can Satan cast out Satan? If I drive out demons by Beelzebub, by whom do your sons cast them out?" With His words, He exposed the absurdity of their claim, reminding them that division is a path to destruction, and that attributing the power of God to evil was a dangerous game. (Matthew 12:25-27)

He continued, "But if I cast out demons by the Spirit of God, then the Kingdom of God has come upon you." Here, Jesus asserted His divine authority, signifying that His miracles were not mere magic but the manifestation of the Eternal One's power on earth. (Matthew 12:28)

Illustrating the gravity of His mission, He added, "How can one enter a strong man's house and plunder his goods unless he first binds the strong man?" By this, He intimated that His power was superior even to that of the devil, the so-called "strong man" of the earth. Jesus was the stronger one, capable of binding evil and restoring the balance of light. (Matthew 12:29)

In a concluding note of warning, a challenge to all present, Jesus declared, "He who is not with Me is against Me, and he who does not gather with Me scatters." His words drew a distinct line in the sands of time, urging all to choose their allegiance wisely—for in the cosmic battle of good versus evil, neutrality was not an option. (Matthew 12:30)

The Unforgivable Sin: A Line Crossed

Amidst the murmurs of the crowd and the ever-darkening expressions of the Pharisees, the atmosphere became thick with tension. The religious elite, prideful and steeped in their self-made traditions, could not fathom the miraculous power Jesus displayed. Instead of acknowledging the divine at work, they clung to their disdain, attributing Jesus'

deeds to Beelzebub—the prince of demons. (Matthew 12:24)

Jesus, perceiving the depths of their hearts and the weight of their blasphemy, addressed them. His voice was firm, yet filled with an underlying sorrow, knowing the gravity of their spiritual condition. "All manner of sin and blasphemy shall be forgiven unto men, but the blasphemy against the Holy Ghost shall not be forgiven unto men," He proclaimed. His words conveyed a profound truth—the temporality of the flesh, and the contrast with the eternal nature of the Spirit. While insults thrown at a man could be pardoned, mocking the very essence and power of God was a transgression of an entirely different magnitude. (Matthew 12:31-32)

"Either make the tree good, and his fruit good; or else make the tree corrupt, and his fruit corrupt: for the tree is known by his fruit." With these words, Jesus unveiled a universal principle. Just as a tree is identified by the fruit it bears, so is the heart of a person revealed through their words and actions. He was challenging the Pharisees—and everyone present—to introspect, to recognize the state of their inner being. (Matthew 12:33)

But the Master Teacher didn't stop there. "You brood of vipers! How can your words ever ring with truth when your hearts are steeped in falsehood?" Jesus remarked. With these stinging words, He revealed their lineage—not of Abraham or Moses, but of the ancient deceiver, the serpent. Their malice, evident in their words against the Spirit, was a reflection of this very lineage, a lineage that stood in stark contrast to the eternal truths of the I AM. (Matthew 12:34)

The Power of the Spoken Word

The atmosphere, thick with tension, seemed to pulsate with the weight of what had transpired. The Pharisees, so blinded by their fears and prejudices, failed to discern the divine power that flowed through Jesus. Instead, they painted it as the craft of Beelzebub. Jesus, with a deep insight that pierced through their facades, continued to unveil deeper truths about the essence of words and the reflection of the heart.

Not one to be cowed, Jesus looked them directly in their eyes, the depth of His gaze reaching into the very essence of their beings. "Understand this," He began, "a man of true Faith, whom the Eternal One deems 'good,' has a treasury within him. From it, he draws forth words of hope, love, and affirmation — words that mirror the promises of the I AM. On the contrary, one whose heart is gripped by fear, devoid of Faith, will only spew forth venom, drawing from a storehouse of trepidation and deceit." The stark contrast was laid bare: while the faithful echoed God's affirmations, the Pharisees' words, tainted by their alignment with the old serpent, only resonated with negativity. (Matthew 12:35)

"But heed my warning," Jesus continued, his voice echoing through the stone-laden streets, "every idle word, every utterance void of the Spirit's power and essence, will be held to account." He was clear in His message: Words weren't just mere sounds, they were potent seeds. Seeds which, when planted, bore fruit — either of righteousness or of decay. (Matthew 12:36)

He concluded with a profound truth that resonated with all who heard, "By your words, you'll be justified, and by them, you'll be condemned." Each word spoken, whether in Faith or in fear, would determine one's destiny. Words of Faith, reflecting God's promises, had the power to redeem and justify, while words of fear and deceit would only bring about one's downfall. (Matthew 12:37)

The Quest for Signs

Some among them, with veiled mockery in their tones, called out, "Master, show us a sign!" They yearned for a theatrical display, a visible proof of His divine origin. Casting out demons, healing the sick — these wonders weren't enough. Their hearts, clouded by doubt and skepticism, clamored for more. (Matthew 12:38)

Jesus, perceiving their true intent, responded with a sorrowful sigh. "An adulterous generation you are," He began. This was not just an accusation of marital infidelity but a spiritual one. The people of Israel were God's bride, and by seeking after other gods and rejecting the signs already before them, they were committing spiritual adultery. "You seek a sign, but no sign will be given to you except the sign of the prophet Jonah." The crowd murmured, intrigued by the reference to one of their own storied prophets. (Matthew 12:39)

He continued, the weight of His words sinking deep into the hearts of those present, "For as Jonah was three days and three nights in the belly of the great fish, so will the Son of Man be three days and three nights in the heart of the earth." The very core of the Earth would bear witness to the most epic event in human history: the death and resurrection of the Son of God. (Matthew 12:40)

"But there's more," Jesus said, His gaze piercing through the crowd. "The men of Nineveh, who heeded Jonah's call and repented, will rise at the judgment and condemn this generation." Jesus' message was clear. The Gentiles, once deemed outsiders by the Jews, would stand as a testimony to faith and repentance, while many among the chosen people remained obstinate and unyielding. (Matthew 12:41)

He then conjured the tale of a determined queen — the Queen of the South. "She traveled from the ends of the earth to hear the wisdom of Solomon. But here, in your midst, stands One greater than Solomon!" The message was unmistakable. The wisest king had once held court in Jerusalem, but now, Wisdom incarnate walked its streets, offering truths more profound than any Solomon had ever uttered. (Matthew 12:42)

The crowd was left in awe, pondering the gravity of Jesus' words, while the Pharisees and scribes were silenced, their schemes thwarted by the profound wisdom of the Son of God.

The Haunting of the Vacant Soul

As the discourse of the Queen of the South and Jonah's sign resonated through the minds of the listeners, a pregnant pause filled the air. The scribes and Pharisees, still grappling with the weight of Jesus' words and the implications of the signs, were preparing yet another retort. But Jesus, always one step ahead, continued His discourse on the spiritual truths of the Kingdom.

He spoke with a depth of insight that cut through the superficiality of ritualistic faith, "When the impure spirit has departed from a person, it wanders through desolate regions in search of rest but finds none." The eyes of many in the crowd widened. They were familiar with the rituals of cleansing, but Jesus

was introducing a deeper dimension. An exorcism was not the end; it was merely the beginning of a spiritual journey. (Matthew 12:43)

Jesus went on, His voice ringing with a mixture of caution and compassion, "Then it says, 'I will return to my former dwelling,' and upon its return, it discovers the house to be empty, clean, and adorned." Those who had witnessed or experienced exorcisms felt a chill down their spine. The spiritual realm, as described by Jesus, was not as simple as they had once believed. Merely evicting an evil spirit was not enough; something had to fill that void. (Matthew 12:44)

Drawing them deeper into the ramifications of this truth, Jesus added, "It then goes and gathers seven other spirits even more malevolent than itself, and together they enter and make their home there. The final condition of that individual is worse than the initial one." The crowd gasped. The stakes of the spiritual warfare were higher than they'd imagined. The heart, once purified, was a battleground where vigilance was paramount. (Matthew 12:45)

The imagery was clear: just as the Pharisees demanded signs and were not content with the miracles they had witnessed, an empty soul would always seek more, often to its own peril. True spiritual fulfillment was not in the mere absence of evil but in the presence of the Divine.

The onlookers were confronted with a new realization: The spiritual life was not a passive one. It was a constant endeavor to fill oneself with the virtues and spirit of the Divine, lest the void attract darker forces. This revelation, layered on top of Jesus' prior teachings, left an indelible mark on all who heard. The path to righteousness was clearer, but it was also evident that diligence and genuine faith were paramount.

The Boundless Family of Faith

As the echoes of Jesus' teachings on spiritual warfare continued to reverberate, a sudden commotion on the edge of the crowd brought a new focus. There, trying to make their way to the heart of the assembly, were members of Jesus' own family. Word had reached them of the intense confrontations Jesus had been facing, and out of concern, they had come to see Him. (Matthew 12:46)

A man from the crowd, possibly recognizing the familiar faces, brought it to Jesus' attention, "Look, your mother and your brothers are waiting outside, wanting to speak with you" The crowd shifted, many expecting Jesus to cease His teachings and greet His family. However, Jesus, ever the Master of moments, turned the situation into a profound teaching moment.

But, instead of rushing to their side, He gestured towards His disciples, declaring, "Who is my mother? And who are my brothers?" He then stretched forth His hand toward his disciples, a symbolic gesture, and proclaimed, "Behold my mother and my brothers! For anyone who does the will of my Father in heaven is like a brother, sister, and mother to me." (Matthew 12:48-50)

This was a profound declaration. Jesus wasn't denying His biological family, but He was expanding the concept of family to something grander, a spiritual family that transcended blood and lineage. In the Kingdom of Heaven, bonds were forged not by birthright, but by faith and shared purpose.

As the sun set on that pivotal day, the teachings of Jesus, both confrontational and comforting, lingered in the hearts of those who heard. From challenges to the Pharisees to lessons of spiritual vigilance, and finally to the definition of the true family of faith, Jesus painted a vivid picture of the Kingdom of Heaven. Those who listened were left with a choice — to continue in old ways or to embrace the transformative call of the Messiah. The stage was set for even greater revelations and miracles, as the journey of Jesus and His disciples pressed on into the annals of history.

CHAPTER 13

THE PARABLES OF THE KINGDOM

A New Dawn of Wisdom

With the first brushstrokes of dawn painting the sky, Jesus stood ready to cast the seeds of heavenly wisdom into the fertile hearts of those gathered. As the Master of Parables, He would weave a narrative tapestry, revealing the hidden facets of the Kingdom through stories steeped in the mundane yet brimming with the mystical. The new day heralded more than the sun's rise; it promised an illumination of the spirit, as parables would unfold the mysteries of the ages to those with ears to hear and eyes to see.

Whispers by the Seashore

As dawn's early light spilled over the ancient city of Capernaum, Jesus emerged from a humble dwelling, the home of Simon Peter—a fisherman turned disciple. With each step toward the shores of the Sea of Galilee, the weight of His mission pressed upon Him. The sea stretched out like a vast mirror, reflecting the deep blues of the heavens, interrupted only by the gentle ripples caused by the morning breeze. (Matthew 13:1)

As Jesus approached the water's edge, the sands became a mosaic of eager souls—men, women, children, merchants, fishermen, and more—all drawn to the enigmatic teacher. Their murmurs, a blend of cu-

riosity and expectation, merged with the distant calls of seagulls. The scene was so overwhelming that Jesus made a choice to set foot on a boat, anchoring it just off the coast. The masses settled along the beach, eyes fixed on Him, creating an amphitheater of anticipation. From His vantage point on the boat, Jesus could see the entirety of the gathered crowd, their faces a canvas of hope and wonder. (Matthew 13:2)

Taking a deep breath, feeling the cool, salty air filling His lungs, Jesus began to unfold the divine secrets of the Eternal One's kingdom. He started not with a direct teaching or command but with a story—a parable. The tale was of a sower, a timeless representation of any farmer in the land of Israel. But the listeners would soon realize that this was no ordinary story. This was a narrative dripping with spiritual truths, meant to challenge, provoke, and enlighten. (Matthew 13:3)

He spoke of the sower who went out to sow. As he scattered the seeds, some fell by the wayside, becoming fodder for the birds that swooped down hungrily. Some seeds landed on stony places, where they sprouted quickly but, lacking depth of soil, withered under the scorching sun. Others fell among thorns, which grew with them, eventually choking their vitality. Yet, there were seeds that found their way to good ground, flourishing and producing a harvest beyond imagination—some a hundredfold, some sixty, and some thirty (Matthew 13:4-8).

As the story settled in the minds of the listeners, a hush descended. They sensed the gravity of what they'd just heard. This was not just about a sower and seeds; it was a mirror to their souls, a call to introspection. How would they respond to the words of the I AM, shared by Jesus? Only time would unveil the mysteries embedded in this parable.

The Unveiling of Secrets

Amidst the gathering, His closest disciples, deeply intrigued and possibly a bit puzzled, approached Him. Their earnestness was evident as they inquired,

"Why do you address them in parables?" (Matthew 13:10) They sought to fathom the depth of Jesus' teachings, hoping to pierce the veil of mystery.

Jesus, recognizing their genuine thirst for knowledge, leaned in and shared a profound truth: "It has been granted to you to comprehend the mysteries of the Kingdom of Heaven, but to them, it has not been given." (Matthew 13:11) Here was a staggering revelation: those genuinely seeking the truth would be granted understanding, but for the skeptical and the hardened, these deeper truths would remain elusive.

He continued, "Whoever possesses, more shall be given to them, and they will have an abundance. But those who do not have, even what they have will be taken away from them." (Matthew 13:12) Those truly seeking, with an open heart and mind, would gain even more insight and understanding. But those who were indifferent or closed off would lose even the little understanding they had.

His voice grew solemn as He continued, "So I speak to them in parables because, even though they see, they do not truly perceive; and though they hear, they do not genuinely understand." (Matthew 13:13) The scene became almost palpable with gravity. There were those amidst the crowd who, though physically present, were spiritually distant. Their hearts, overburdened with prejudices and skepticism, made them blind and deaf to the truths Jesus presented.

The Heart's Echo:
Understanding Spiritual Hardening

In the midst of His profound teachings, Jesus unveiled a deep spiritual reality, echoing the words of the prophet Isaiah. He declared, "For the hearts of this people have become calloused, their ears are slow to hear, and they have closed their eyes. Otherwise, they might see with their eyes, hear with their ears, understand with their hearts, and turn, and I would heal them." (Matthew 13:14-15)

A "calloused heart" is not just a poetic description but a piercing insight into the spiritual state of many. It is the heart that has been overloaded, inundated with the sounds and sights of the world to the point of saturation. Just as clay hardens over time when exposed to the elements, a heart, constantly subjected to worldly influences without the softening touch of divine truths, can harden. This hardness isn't just a physical state but a spiritual condition where the divine message finds it challenging to penetrate, unable to find fertile ground within to take root and flourish.

The "ears slow to hear" paints a vivid image of spiritual fatigue. It's not that these ears cannot hear, but they are burdened, heavy-laden with the incessant noise of worldly affairs, drowning out the gentle whispers of heavenly truths. An individual so bombarded might reach a state where they can't discern the profound from the mundane. The divine melodies that once resonated deep within get lost amidst the cacophony of life's distractions.

The "eyes closed" signify a conscious choice. It's not a mere failure of sight but a willful refusal to acknowledge the light, to see the divine in the everyday. They have become so accustomed to the darkness that the prospect of the light seems daunting. By shutting out this light, they are shutting out the hope of transformation and healing.

Yet, the profound sadness in Jesus' words lies in the missed opportunity. For if only they would genuinely see with their spiritual eyes, listen with their unburdened ears, and understand with a softened heart, they could embrace a transformation like no other. The Word, in all its divine glory, would become effective in their lives, leading them away from their old ways and into the healing embrace of God's truth. The promise is not just of understanding but of con-

version and healing, a return to the original design intended by the Creator.

Yet, in the midst of this somber revelation, Jesus brought hope and encouragement to His disciples, drawing a clear distinction between the masses and them. His voice softened, tinged with pride and gratitude as He looked at His closest followers, "But blessed are your eyes, for they see: and your ears, for they hear." (Matthew 13:16) Their hearts had not hardened; they had chosen to follow Him, to listen intently to His words, to seek understanding. Their eyes beheld wonders and their ears captured divine truths that many prophets and righteous people longed to witness but did not have the opportunity.

"For truly I say unto you," Jesus continued with an intensity that captured their complete attention, "That many prophets and righteous men have desired to see those things which you see, and have not seen them; and to hear those things which you hear, and have not heard them."(Matthew 13:17) Here, Jesus emphasized the unique privilege His disciples had. They were living in a time of divine revelation, witnessing the unfolding of God's redemptive plan firsthand. Their position was enviable, even to the revered prophets of old.

The disciples, sensing the gravity of Jesus' words, realized that their journey with Him wasn't just a privilege but also a responsibility. They were the torchbearers of these truths, the ones chosen to carry forward this message to future generations. The weight of this realization settled deep within their hearts, reinforcing their commitment to their divine Teacher and His mission.

The Sower and the Four Grounds

With the sun high in the sky, casting an amber hue upon the multitude that had gathered, Jesus leaned forward slightly, beckoning the crowd to listen more closely. His voice was calm and inviting, "So, listen carefully to the parable of the sower." (Matthew 13:18) Every eye was fixated on Him, the breeze carrying His words to the farthest listeners.

"When any one hears the word of the Kingdom," He began, alluding to the Eternal One's divine message, "And if they fail to grasp it, the evil one arrives." He paused for emphasis, "And snatches away what was sown in their heart. This represents the one who received the seed along the path." (Matthew 13:19) Jesus painted a vivid picture: the hardened path representing a hardened heart, where the Word—divine, powerful, full of potential—could find no depth. On such ground, the seed lay exposed, vulnerable. The birds, symbols of evil spirits, could easily swoop down and take the seed away, robbing the individual of even the chance to understand the Kingdom's truth.

Moving on to the next scenario, Jesus continued, "But the one who received the seed in the rocky ground is the one who hears the word and immediately welcomes it with joy. Yet, they have no deep roots within, and they endure only for a while. When trouble or persecution arises because of the word, they quickly stumble and fall away." (Matthew 13:20-21) Here, the image was of ground filled with rocks beneath the surface. Although the seed could germinate quickly, the rocks prevented the roots from going deep. These were the people who, upon hearing the Word, show immediate joy but lack depth and stability in their faith. The slightest challenge, the slightest test of their commitment, and they fall away, their shallow roots unable to anchor them.

He took a deep breath before diving into the next imagery, "The one who received the seed among the thorns is the one who hears the word, but the worries of this world and the allure of wealth strangle the word within, making them unproductive." (Matthew 13:22) These words conveyed the image of a ground cluttered with thorns and weeds. Although the seed

starts to grow, the surrounding thorns—representing life's worries, temptations, and the allure of materialism—grow faster and stronger, suffocating the budding plant. The Word is heard but soon overshadowed by the world's seductions.

Concluding this profound teaching, Jesus spoke of the ideal scenario, "But the one who received the seed in the good soil is the one who hears the word, comprehends it, and bears fruit, yielding some a hundredfold, some sixty, and some thirty." (Matthew 13:23) The good ground represented a heart open and receptive, free from obstacles and distractions. In such a heart, the Word not only flourishes but multiplies, bearing fruit that, in turn, becomes seeds to sow elsewhere. This is the transformative power of truly accepting and understanding the divine Word.

The crowd, deeply immersed in the illustrations Jesus provided, began to introspect. Which ground did their heart resemble? The answer to this question would determine the trajectory of their spiritual journey.

The Field of Destiny:
Wheat and Tares Intertwined

As the crowd leaned in, eager for another parable, the distant hum of the sea served as a serene backdrop. Jesus, seeing the inquisitiveness in their eyes, began to unravel a tale that would stir their souls.

"The Kingdom of Heaven," Jesus commenced, casting His gaze over the multitude, "can be compared to a man who planted good seeds in his field." (Matthew 13:24) The imagery was vivid: a vast field under the open sky, filled with potential and promise. The sower, diligently scattering seeds that held life within them. The hope for a bountiful harvest was palpable.

"But while men slept," Jesus continued with a hint of caution in His voice, "his enemy came and sowed tares among the wheat, and went his way." (Matthew 13:25) In the stillness of night, an adversary had introduced imposters into the field—tares that would grow alongside the wheat, almost indistinguishable until the time of harvest. The sinister act was covert, aiming to sabotage the good harvest with these unwelcome invaders.

When the truth of this deception was uncovered, the servants, filled with concern, approached the sow-

er, "Master, did you not sow good seed in your field? How then does it have tares" (Matthew 13:27) Their distress was evident; they had expected an unblemished field, but now faced the challenge of intertwined wheat and tares.

The sower, discerning the deeper implications, responded, "An enemy has done this." Recognizing the heart of their concern, he advised, "Let both grow together until the harvest: and in the time of harvest I will say to the reapers, Gather the tares first and bind them in bundles to burn them, but gather the wheat into my barn." (Matthew 13:28-30)

Jesus painted a picture of ultimate discernment and judgment. The wisdom of the sower was clear: a premature attempt to uproot the tares might also uproot the wheat. Both needed time to fully grow, to show their true nature. At the appointed time, there would be a clear distinction between the two. The wheat, a symbol of the righteous, would be safely stored, while the tares, representing the wicked, would face a fiery end.

This profound tale demonstrated the patience of the Divine. While evil persists alongside good in the world, a time will come when each will be treated ac-

cording to its nature. The righteous will be rewarded, and the wicked will face consequences.

For the listeners, the parable was an invitation to self-examination: to consider the seeds they allowed to grow within them and to be patient yet vigilant in their spiritual journey. It was a lesson in discernment, trust in the Divine plan, and the eventual triumph of good over evil.

Epic in its scope, this narrative encapsulated the essence of the human experience — the interplay of light and dark, good and evil. Through it, Jesus not only conveyed spiritual truths about the Kingdom of Heaven but also offered profound insights into the challenges and triumphs that each soul would encounter on its journey.

The Kingdom's Growth: From the Minuscule to the Monumental

In the gentle ebb and flow of His teachings, Jesus turned the attention of His listeners to something seemingly insignificant: a mustard seed.

Another parable put he forth unto them, saying, "The Kingdom of Heaven is akin to a mustard seed, a man took and sowed in his field. Although it is the smallest of all seeds, when it grows, it becomes the

largest of shrubs, even a tree, so that the birds of the air come and nest in its branches."(Matthew 13:31-32)

This vivid imagery imparted by Jesus was profound. A mustard seed, in its minuscule form, appears almost inconsequential. Yet, once planted and nurtured, its potential is unleashed, growing into a tree that offers shelter to the birds. Similarly, the Kingdom of Heaven, though it might start with a tiny act of faith or a small gesture of love, can expand into something monumental, touching countless lives.

The Mystical Leaven: Transformation from Within

He told them another parable. "The Kingdom of Heaven is like leaven that a woman took and hid in three measures of flour, till it was all leavened."

Here, Jesus introduces the mysterious workings of leaven (yeast). A little leaven, when mixed with flour, permeates the entire dough, causing it to rise. This transformative power of leaven mirrors the transformative power of the Kingdom of Heaven in the hearts of men and women. Just as a bit of yeast affects the entire batch, so too does the influence of the Kingdom change the entirety of a person's being, radiating outward and influencing the world around them.

Through these parables, Jesus illuminated the dynamic nature of the Kingdom of Heaven. It's not always about grand gestures or monumental acts; sometimes, it's the smallest actions, the tiniest seeds of faith, that lead to the most significant transformations. The message was clear: never underestimate the immense potential that lies in humble beginnings and the deep, inner transformations.

The Parabolic Method: Unveiling the Prophetic Truth

"All these things Jesus spoke to the crowd in parables; He did not speak to them without using parables. This was to fulfill what was spoken by the prophet, saying, 'I will open my mouth in parables; I will reveal hidden things that have been kept secret since the foundation of the world" (Matthew 13:34-35)

In this poignant moment, Jesus' use of parables wasn't just a teaching method; it was a fulfillment of ancient prophecy. The Master Teacher was intentionally unveiling truths in this manner to bring to light secrets preserved since the dawn of creation. Through these illustrative stories, Jesus made profound spiritual truths accessible and relatable to His listeners, while also signaling the greater divine orchestration at play. The narrative of history and prophecy was being unfurled, with Jesus at its very center, revealing mysteries that had been concealed for ages.

The Celestial Harvest: Unveiling the Dual Destiny

In a private setting, away from the masses, Jesus' closest disciples approach Him, yearning for clarity on the mysterious parable of the tares. With compassion and wisdom, the Savior delves into its depths, unraveling the tapestry of eternal significance that lies within.

Jesus begins, "He that sows the good seed is the Son of Man;" (Matthew 13:37) Right from the outset, He identifies Himself as the divine sower, emphasizing His intimate involvement in the spiritual growth of humanity.

The field, He explains, represents the world, a vast expanse filled with myriad souls. The good seeds that sprout into wheat signify the righteous, while the tares, sown by the enemy, depict the children of wickedness. This adversary is none other than the devil, the age-old deceiver, forever in opposition to God's divine plan.

But the climax of this narrative is yet to come. A time is foretold when the "Son of Man will send forth his angels, and they will gather out of his Kingdom all causes of sin and all the law-breakers." (Matthew 13:41) This divine reaping, reminiscent of a cosmic harvest, will see the righteous and the wicked separated, much like the wheat from the tares.

The fate of the wicked is a somber one. Cast into a furnace of fire, there will be "anguished cries and the grinding of teeth." (Matthew 13:42) This graphic portrayal serves as a stark warning, highlighting the gravity of one's choices on earth and their eternal consequences.

But for the righteous, the promise is one of re-splendent glory: they shall shine forth as the sun in the

Kingdom of their Father, an eternal testament to God's mercy, grace, and love.

In this profound revelation, Jesus underscores the dual destiny awaiting humanity. The cosmic war between good and evil will culminate in a decisive victory for righteousness. Those who align themselves with the Son of Man will bask in eternal radiance, while those who choose the path of wickedness will face dire consequences.

With a tone of urgency, Jesus leaves His listeners with a compelling call to discernment, for those with ears, let them hear and choose their destiny wisely.

The Treasures of the Kingdom

With the sunset painting the sky in hues of divine grace, Jesus, the benevolent teacher, further unveiled the treasures of the kingdom with a pair of brief yet profound parables. "Again, the Kingdom of Heaven is compared to treasure hidden in a field; which a man found and covered up and hid it. Then in his joy he goes and sells all that he has, and buys that field,." (Matthew 13:44)

The metaphor, as simple as it was, carried within it the essence of the eternal quest, a narrative of sacrifice, and unfathomable joy in the discovery of the divine kingdom. The quest for the Eternal One was not a journey laden with materialistic gains, but a venture of the spirit, diving into the fathomless ocean of divine love and wisdom.

The teaching continued as Jesus drew another gem from the treasure of divine knowledge, "Once more, the Kingdom of Heaven is like a merchant seeking fine pearls. When he found one pearl of great value, he went and sold all he possessed to acquire it." (Matthew 13:45-46)

The Grand Finale:
Lessons from the Seashore

From the onset of dawn, beside the calm sea, Jesus had been weaving tales of divine truths. With every passing parable, from the sower's seeds to the hidden

treasure, the audience found themselves captivated. Their eyes fixed upon Him, they stood on the sandy shores as He sat comfortably in a boat, creating an intimate theater between the Teacher and the taught. The sun now hung a little lower, casting longer shadows and painting the water with hues of gold.

He began again, drawing from the vast expanse before Him, "Once more, the Kingdom of Heaven is like a net that was cast into the sea and gathered fish of every kind." (Matthew 13:47) For the fishermen in the crowd, this imagery was all too familiar, yet beneath the surface lay profound truths about the Kingdom of Heaven.

As the net indiscriminately captures, so too does the embrace of the Divine Realm. Yet, as every fisherman knows, the final catch needs sorting. Here, Jesus unveiled a divine promise: "This is how it will be at the end of the world: the angels will come forth and separate the wicked from the righteous,." (Matthew 13:49) A potent message of a time when the righteous and wicked will be discerned and met with respective destinies.

Jesus concluded, drawing a comparison between the learned scribes of the Kingdom and a wise homeowner: "So, every scholar well-versed in the ways of

the Kingdom of Heaven is like a homeowner who brings out from his treasure both new and old treasures." (Matthew 13:52) The scholars of divine truths, He explained, value both ancient wisdom and new insights, drawing from both in their quest for understanding.

As the sun began its descent, casting a warm glow over the sea and shore, Jesus' discourse by the seaside reached its grand finale. Those who came seeking wisdom left with their souls enriched, their minds opened to truths profound yet elegantly simple. The waves whispered their approval, the sand bore witness, and the sun bid adieu, signaling the end of a day when the Teacher, seated in His boat, shared with the world parables that would resonate through the ages.

Homecoming Shadows: The Hometown Prophet

As the amber horizon gave way to twilight's embrace, Jesus disembarked from the vessel that had been His pulpit. With the sands of the beach beneath His feet and the memories of the day's lessons echoing in the hearts of many, He ventured towards Nazareth, the place of His upbringing.

The air in Nazareth was thick with anticipation. The local boy, now a man of profound wisdom and miraculous power, had returned. The murmurs grew louder as He entered the synagogue, sharing with fervor the wisdom that God had bestowed upon Him. "Where does this man acquire such wisdom and perform these miraculous deeds?" they marveled. (Matthew 13:54)

For the Nazarenes, Jesus was no stranger. They remembered Him as the carpenter's son, a memory fortified by the mention of Joseph, the man who might have played a pivotal role in His early life. Familiarity, as they say, breeds contempt. They knew of Mary, His mother, and they recounted His brothers - James, Joses, Simon, Judas - and spoke of His sisters. The ties of kinship, which should have been a bond of trust, became a shackle of doubt.

A bitter undercurrent simmered through the marvel. "Is not this the carpenter's son?" they questioned. (Matthew 13:55) "And his sisters, are they not all with us?" There was a scandalizing disbelief, a stumbling block that tripped many in Nazareth. Their doubt was palpable. How could someone they had seen grow, play, and live amongst them now command such authority and wisdom?

In their questions lay not just skepticism but an impediment to faith. They were "offended" in Him - skandalizō - as if His very presence and teachings became a stumbling block, causing many to distrust, to desert, and to judge Him unjustly. His authority was challenged not by His words or actions but by their preconceived perceptions.

It was heartbreaking and profoundly ironic. Here was Jesus, the source of eternal salvation, and yet in His own homeland, His hands were tied. Not by the might of armies or the decree of kings, but by the disbelief of those He had come to save. The very lack of faith, a chasm of doubt, prevented many miracles from manifesting. "And he did not many mighty works there because of their unbelief,." (Matthew 13:58)

And so, in the twilight of Nazareth, a lesson emerged - one that transcended time and space: faith, or the lack thereof, is the catalyst. The very force that can summon miracles can also silence them, solely based on the condition of the heart.

CHAPTER 14

THE
DANCE OF FATE

The Ripple of Divine Teachings

As the dawn cast a golden veil over the land, the residents of Galilee found themselves in the throes of a revelation, the echoes of Jesus' parables from the day before still resounding through the hills and valleys. The essence of divine knowledge had begun to seep into hearts, stirring the waters of understanding and anticipation for the teachings yet to come...

Herod's Dismay and The Ghost of Guilt

In the shadowed halls of power, where opulence and decadence danced hand in hand, Herod Antipas, the tetrarch, presided over his birthday feast, a spectacle of excess and revelry. Yet, beneath the surface of merriment and wine-soaked laughter, a shiver of fear coursed through him. Murmurs had reached his ears, tales not of John, whom he had confined in chains, but of Jesus, whose miraculous deeds stirred the people. They spoke in hushed tones, wondering aloud if this was John the Baptist reborn from the dead, manifesting powers that challenged the very nature of their reality. (Matthew 14:1-2)

Caught in the grip of his own superstitions, Herod's mind was haunted by the thought of John's righteous spirit, rising in defiance. He remembered with a grimace the desert prophet's biting words that had lacerated his soul, condemning his illicit union with Herodias, his brother's wife. The echo of that holy man's voice, now mingled with the talk of Jesus's wonders, gnawed at the edges of his conscience. (Matthew 14:3-4)

As wine flowed and music swelled within the palace walls, Salome, Herodias's daughter, spun and twirled before the assembly with such grace that even the cold-hearted Herod found himself spellbound. In a reckless oath, he pledged to grant her heart's desire, up to half his kingdom, caught in the web of her beguiling dance. Unbeknownst to him, a sinister plot was about to unfold, whispered from the lips of a vindictive Herodias into the ear of her innocent daughter. (Matthew 14:6-7)

With the solemnity of a death knell, Salome voiced the demand that would forever mar the night, "Serve me here the head of John the Baptist on a platter." A chill swept the room, and Herod's blood ran cold. Trapped by his own vow and the eyes of his court, he ordered the execution. In the darkness of the dungeon, the blade fell, and the voice that once cried in the wilderness was silenced. John's disciples mourned as they buried their mentor, and with heavy hearts, they departed to share the somber tidings with Jesus. (Matthew 14:8-12)

From the depths of a gruesome feast to the whispers of a rumored resurrection, the tale of John's end was but the beginning of a new chapter, one where light would soon confront the shadows, and the mission of the one they called Jesus would unfurl across the land.

Upon the Shores of Compassion

As the shadow of grief for John's brutal end enveloped Jesus, He sought the solace of solitude. The somber news drove Him to a place apart, a quiet refuge across the still waters of the Sea of Galilee, to commune with the Father and to mourn. Yet, even in His quest for quietude, the masses yearned for His presence, their hearts a sea of needs and hopes. Upon hearing the whispers of His departure, they followed on foot from the towns, their figures dotting the shoreline like a living mosaic. (Matthew 14:13)

When Jesus, crossing the water's gentle embrace, beheld the multitude, His heart was stirred. The veil of His own sorrow was lifted by the sight of their eager faces; their ailments and afflictions called out to Him. And so, in the midst of His personal loss, Jesus extended the hands of healing, and they, in turn, were made whole. (Matthew 14:14)

As the day waned and the sky painted itself in the hues of twilight, the disciples came to Him, their voices laden with practical concern, "This is a deserted place, and the hour is already late. Send the crowds away, that they may go into the villages and buy themselves food." But Jesus, perceiving a moment ripe for faith to manifest, challenged them, "They do not need to leave; you can provide them with something to eat." (Matthew 14:15-16)

With the setting sun as their backdrop, the disciples' bewildered expressions spoke volumes. "We have here only five loaves and two fishes," they answered. What were these among so many? Yet, in the hands of the Master, scarcity would soon unfold into abundance. (Matthew 14:17)

Jesus, with divine intention, bid the gathered souls to rest upon the green tapestry of grass. With the five loaves and two fishes cradled reverently in His hands, He lifted His eyes heavenward. In that serene moment, with the hush of expectancy over the crowd, He offered a prayer of gratitude that resonated with the ancient echoes of faith, "Blessed are You, Lord our God, King of the universe, who brings forth bread from the earth." He then broke the bread, His actions deliberate, infusing the simple meal with the fullness of divine blessing. The disciples, taking the sanctified offering, wove through the assembly, and the food multiplied miraculously with each portion they shared. What was scarce became plentiful, a testament to the boundless generosity of the kingdom, as every person ate and was satisfied. When the remnants were gathered, twelve baskets stood, brimming—a silent witness to the day's wonder. (Matthew 14:18-21)

In the wake of loss, a new story of hope and provision was written upon the shores of Galilee. Jesus had turned mourning into a miracle, showing that in the Kingdom of Heaven, compassion knows no bounds, and faith has the power to feed the multitudes.

The Sovereign Amidst the Storm

The Sea of Galilee, shrouded in the cloak of night, became a theatre of divine revelation. As the disciples, seasoned men of the waters, toiled against the tempest's wrath, their Master sought solace on a distant hill, His prayers ascending to the heavens where stars kept silent vigil. Little did they know, their faith was about to be forged in the crucible of the supernatural. (Matthew 14:22-23)

The night, wearing on towards the watch when even soldiers at their posts feel the weight of weariness, found the disciples far from shore. Here, the rebellion of creation itself was a roaring declaration against their presence. The wind's howl and the waves' ire spoke of an ancient chaos, unrestrained and merciless. (Matthew 14:24)

Then, in the heart of the maelstrom, a form appeared—a silhouette against the tumult, an impossibility made flesh. Upon the water He walked, as one might stroll through a calm garden, untouched by the fury around Him. To the disciples' fear-filled eyes, this could only be a specter, a ghostly omen amidst their struggle for survival. (Matthew 14:25-26)

His voice, however, was no ethereal whisper. It cut through the roar of the elements, a clear, resonant call to courage, "Be of good cheer; it is I; be not afraid." It was the voice of the I AM, the eternal constant, whose very essence was the antithesis of fear. (Matthew 14:27)

Amidst the terrified crew, Peter, a man whose heart was as tumultuous as the sea he faced, issued a challenge to the impossible. "Lord, if it is truly You, 'he exclaimed,' command me to come to You on the water." And in response, a single word from Jesus shattered the boundaries of reality, "Come." With that command, Peter stepped into the realm of faith made visible. (Matthew 14:28-29)

But as the wind snarled like a cornered beast, Peter's focus wavered, and with it, his miraculous stance upon the waves. Fear, that ancient adversary, clawed at his conviction, dragging him towards the abyss. Yet, his faith, though as frail as a flickering candle, invoked the name of Jesus. Swiftly, mercifully, Jesus' hand grasped his, pulling him from the depths. "O you of little faith," Jesus admonished, "Why did you doubt?" A gentle rebuke, laden with life's deepest lesson. (Matthew 14:30-31)

As they climbed back into the vessel, the chaos bowed to calm, the wind's roar fading to a docile breeze. This was no mere stilling of a storm, but a display of sovereignty over the primal forces of earth. In awe, the disciples prostrated, their hearts ablaze with the realization that before them stood more than a man—He was the living conduit of the Divine. "Truly you are the Son of God," they proclaimed, a declaration born not of sight, but of spirit, as they beheld the master of creation in their midst. (Matthew 14:32-33)

On that fateful night, as the Sea of Galilee bore witness, faith transcended understanding, and the disciples' eyes were opened to the true nature of their Master—a nature that commanded the very elements, that offered His hand in our darkest hour, and called us to walk upon the waters of our fears.

The Haven of Healing

In the tender embrace of early morning, the shores of Gennesaret emerged from the night's shadow, gilded by the daybreak's light. The boat carrying Jesus and His disciples glided over the now-tranquil waters, reaching land just as the sun crowned the horizon with its resplendent light. The recent tempest of fear and wonder still echoed in their spirits, yet here they were, stepping onto the shores where the imminent dawn promised new revelations and healings. (Matthew 14:34)

The people of Gennesaret, stirred by the whispers of dawn, soon recognized the figure of Jesus, whose fame as a healer and teacher had been sown like the first seeds of the day across the lands. A fervent hope began to stir in their hearts, an anticipation that surged with the sun's ascent. They hastened to spread the word, to bring the sick and weary to Him, believing, trusting in the restoration that His mere presence could bring. (Matthew 14:35)

As the early light washed over them, every person brought forth seemed to emerge from the shadows of their ailments into the healing embrace of the morning. They beseeched Him, just to touch the hem of His garment, for even such fleeting contact promised

release and renewal. And true to their faith, as the sun climbed higher and the day grew warm, those who touched were made perfectly whole, a testimony to the mercy that flowed from Him like a never-ending stream. (Matthew 14:36)

In the golden morning, by the shores of Gennesaret, as the world awakened to the rhythm of a day anew, Jesus walked among them — a beacon of hope, a testament to the dawn of healing that had arrived with Him.

CHAPTER 15

THE SWORD
OF
TRUTH

From Gennesaret's Grace to Pharisaic Confrontation

The gentle waves of Gennesaret had barely ceased their caress of the humble vessel, which bore Jesus and His disciples, when the news of His arrival spread like wildfire through the regions beyond. It was a tale of hope, borne on the wings of those who had been touched by His healing, reaching far and wide, even to the ears of the Pharisees and scribes in distant Jerusalem. With each narrative, the flame of inquiry and disdain grew, fanned by the unseen winds of fear and challenge to their stronghold of religious rigidity.

Confrontation with Tradition

The sun had scarcely begun its daily ascent when a group of Pharisees and scribes, the purported guardians of religious orthodoxy, approached Jesus. With a facade of respect hiding a core of confrontation, they launched their accusation. "Why do your disciples break the tradition of the elders? They do not wash their hands before they eat bread." They voiced, their words filled with the ice of accusation, a stark contrast to the warmth that Jesus' teachings usually brought forth. (Matthew 15:1-2)

Jesus, discerning the heart behind the superficial reverence, responded, not with a mere answer but with a question that aimed to pierce the veil of their hypocrisy. "Why do you also violate the command of God with your tradition?" He retorted, His words sharp as the blade of truth cutting through the murky clouds of deceit. He then exposed the core of their transgression, which made void the Word of God through their tradition, highlighting the commandment concerning honoring father and mother which they conveniently sidestepped for the sake of their tradition. The indictment was clear, their purported piety was but a guise for ungodly practices. (Matthew 15:3-6)

With a courage born of divine authority, Jesus further unveiled the hypocrisy of the Pharisees and scribes. Quoting the prophet Isaiah, He shone the light of truth onto their darkened understanding.

"These people come close to me with their words and honor me with their lips, but their hearts are distant from me. Their worship is empty, for they teach as doctrines the commandments of men." The words, a searing indictment, were like a sword separating bone from marrow, tradition from truth. His rebuke against their traditions which strayed from God's commandments left an indelible impression on the crowd that had gathered, their hearts now questioning the authenticity of the teachings of the Pharisees and scribes. (Matthew 15:7-9)

The Defining of Defilement

The Pharisees, in their self-righteous shell, were offended. Yet, Jesus, undeterred, turned to the crowds, His words now a gentle stream of education flowing towards the eager hearts of the listeners. He defined what defiles a man, not the unwashed hands but the unclean thoughts and deeds. The juxtaposition was clear - while the Pharisees harped on external cleanliness, Jesus pointed to the purity of the heart. His words were an exposition of spiritual truth against ritualistic tradition. (Matthew 15:10-20)

The disciples, however, were concerned. "Do you know that the Pharisees were offended, after they heard this saying?" they queried, their faces mirroring their unease. Jesus, in His serene manner, elucidated, "Every plant, which my heavenly Father has not planted, shall be rooted up." His words were a promise and a prophecy - the uprooting of false doctrines and the fall of those blind leaders who, in their ignorance, lead others into pits of falsehood. The seed of truth He was planting was destined to flourish, while the weeds of false tradition were marked for destruction. (Matthew 15:12-14)

The Enlightenment on Defilement

As the disciples gathered around Jesus, amidst the growing murmurs of the crowd, the questions within them brimmed to the surface. Peter, ever the spokesman of the disciples, ventured forth with a query that reflected the bewilderment among them. "Explain to us this parable," Peter implored, seeking clarity amidst the challenging discourse that had just transpired with the Pharisees. His eyes bore the earnest desire for understanding, much like the thirst of a parched land for rain. (Matthew 15:15)

Jesus looked upon His disciples with a blend of patience and exhortation. He addressed their inquiry, gently chiding, "Are you still without understanding?" It was not a rebuke but a call to delve deeper, to rise above the superficial to grasp the spiritual essence. He then elucidated the profound simplicity of the concept - that which enters a man from outside cannot defile him, but what emanates from his heart, these are the bearers of defilement. His explanation flowed like a river of understanding, quenching the thirst of inquiry, bearing away the debris of confusion, and laying bare the bedrock of divine truth. (Matthew 15:16-17)

He further expounded, listing the various outflows of a corrupt heart – evil thoughts, murders, adulteries, fornications, thefts, false witness, blasphemies. Each word pierced the stillness around, like a stone casting ripples upon the calm waters of a lake, the impact of His words revealing the source of true defilement. The contrast between external observances and internal purity was starkly drawn, exposing the shallowness of Pharisaic traditions. The hearts of the disci-

ples and the crowd were stirred, the scales of misinterpretation falling away from their eyes, revealing a clearer perception of righteousness and sin. (Matthew 15:18-20)

The session by the seashore morphed into a platform of divine revelation, the words of Jesus challenging the established norms, and urging a soul-search towards purity. The crowd, once bound by the shackles of traditional observances, now saw a glimpse of the freedom that came with understanding the heart of the Law, over mere adherence to its letter.

The disciples, too, experienced a deepening of insight, as the gentle waves of Gennesaret seemed to echo the wisdom of Jesus, urging them to cast their nets deeper into the spiritual waters of understanding. Each word of Jesus was like a precious pearl, and they, like diligent divers, sought to delve into the depths to retrieve the treasures of heavenly wisdom, each revelation equipping them for the inevitable challenges and confrontations that lay ahead.

A Canaanite's Cry and a Miracle's Manifestation

As the sun journeyed its celestial path, Jesus and His disciples made their way into the coasts of Tyre and Sidon, lands rich with a history of interaction and conflict with the tribes of Israel. The cool breeze carried whispers of the sea's ancient tales, as the troupe ventured into territories less frequented. Among the shadows of these cities once mighty, now mingling with the dust of time, emerged a figure of desperation and hope -- a Canaanite woman. Her presence was a testament to the long-standing rift between her people and the children of Israel, yet her heart bore the insignia of faith strong enough to bridge the ancient chasm. (Matthew 15:21)

The Cry of Desperation

The woman's voice trembled with the anguish and earnestness as she cried out, "Have mercy on me, O Lord, thou Son of David; my daughter is severely tormented by an evil spirit." Her plea soared above the city's murmur, piercing the veil of indifference that history and hatred had sewn between their peoples. Her acknowledgement of Jesus as the 'Son of David' was an anthem of faith, echoing across the disciples' hearts, reverberating through the annals of prejudice and contempt. (Matthew 15:22)

However, in response to her desperate plea, there was silence from the Master. A silence that, to some, seemed to reflect the historical disdain between Israelites and Canaanites. His disciples, perhaps uncomfortable or even irritated by the woman's incessant cries, urged Jesus to send her away. Their words revealed the biases of old, yet Jesus' next move was to redefine boundaries, to challenge the inherited prejudices that even His close followers harbored. (Matthew 15:23)

Faith Beyond Borders

Finally, Jesus spoke, His words seemed initially to reflect the traditional narrative, stating His mission towards the lost sheep of Israel. But the woman, undeterred, threw herself at His feet in worship, making a final plea for her afflicted child. Her persistence was like a fragrant offering, showcasing a faith undeterred by historical enmity or discouraging responses. And then, with a tone of admiration and divine love, Jesus declared her faith as 'great'. In that moment, the ancient walls of division crumbled before the magnitude of her faith as Jesus affirmed, "Woman, your faith is remarkable. Let it be done for you just as you desire." And her daughter was made whole from that very hour, a testament to a faith that transcended boundaries, a living epistle of the limitless love and mercy of the I AM. (Matthew 15:24-28)

The tale of this Canaanite woman, knitted into the grand tapestry of the divine narrative, remains a profound exposition of faith's power to transcend historical, cultural, and racial barriers. It marked a moment of divine revelation, not just for the crowds, but significantly, for the disciples, illuminating the boundless realm of grace awaiting those whose faith dared to break free from the shackles of tradition and prejudice.

From Compassion to Manifestation: The Multitudes Fed

Jesus, with a heart laden with love and eyes that see beyond the mundane, continued His divine journey alongside His disciples. Their feet kissed the dusty trails leading to the Sea of Galilee. As they ascended the mountain, Jesus sat down, and like moths to a flame, multitudes were drawn towards the aura of hope that enveloped Him. They brought with them the sick, the lame, the blind, and the mute, laying them at His feet. Their faith was a plea for the touch of the Divine, a whisper of hope in the face of adversity. (Matthew 15:29-30)

A Cascade of Miracles

As Jesus stretched forth His hands, the mountain reverberated with a symphony of miracles. The mute began to speak, the crippled gained strength, the lame walked, and the blind saw. The fabric of despair was torn apart, making way for the dawn of hope and divine love. Each touch, each word from Jesus, was like a balm to the wounded souls. The cries of anguish turned into an anthem of praise and wonder, glorifying the God of Israel, the Eternal One. (Matthew 15:31)

The Concern of Sustenance

As the day aged, the disciples, concerned, approached Jesus. They were in a wilderness, and the veil of night was soon to descend. The hunger of the multitudes was a tune that played in the hearts of the disciples, yet the question of sustenance in such desolate environs perplexed them. They had but seven loaves and a few little fishes. The disciples, perhaps, had forgotten the miracle of provision they had witnessed not too long ago. (Matthew 15:32-34)

Jesus, perceiving the disciples' apprehension and the needs of the crowd, instructed the multitude to sit down on the ground. With a heart full of divine compassion, He took the seven loaves and the fishes, and after giving thanks to the I AM, He broke them. As He handed them to the disciples, and the disciples to the multitude, a divine multiplication unfolded. It was a feast from heaven, a banquet in the wilderness, a manifest testimony to the divine provision. Every soul was filled, every heart rejoiced in awe of the wondrous provision. (Matthew 15:35-37)

An Emblem of Abundance

From the hands of the Divine, the seven loaves and a few little fishes transformed into an emblem of abundance. The fragments that remained were seven baskets full, a witness to the divine excess, a reflection of the Eternal One's boundless mercy and provision. As the multitude digested the miracle, both in flesh and spirit, a seed of divine revelation was sown in the hearts present. (Matthew 15:37-38)

The episode by the Sea of Galilee was an inscription of divine love and provision, echoing through the corridors of time, whispering to every heart that in the presence of the Divine, scarcity turns into abundance. As Jesus and His disciples bid goodbye to the crowd, they embarked onto a ship, sailing into the heart of the divine narrative that awaited. The rippling waters carried with them the tales of the day, murmuring the saga of love and miracles to the sands of time. (Matthew 15:39)

Chapter 16

The Confrontations and Confessions

The Veil of Ignorance: A Prelude to Enlightenment

In the previous chapter, the scene by the Sea of Galilee left an indelible mark upon the hearts of the disciples and the multitudes. The miracles and the feast manifested from divine compassion reverberated through the hearts as they journeyed forward. The day dawned, bringing with it the winds of confrontation and realization that would stir the very foundations of faith and prophecy.

The Pharisees and Sadducees: A Test of Foresight

With the first light, the grounds of Magdala bore witness to the gathering storm. The Pharisees and Sadducees, enshrouded in their self-righteous cloaks, approached Jesus with hearts hardened and minds sealed to the divine truth. Their request for a sign from heaven was a veneer for their malicious intent to entrap the Son of Man. But Jesus, discerning their hearts, chastised their blindness, pointing to the skies yet laden with the morning hue, and then to the sea, its calmness belying the storms of ignorance that raged in the hearts of the Pharisees and Sadducees. His voice, steady yet stern, resonated through the dense morning air, "When evening comes, you say, 'It will be fair weather, for the sky is red.' And in the morning, 'Today it will be stormy, for the sky is red and overcast.' You hypocrites! You can interpret the appearance of the sky, but can't you discern the signs of the times?" Their countenances paled as the rebuke unveiled their hypocrisy. They had sought a sign, and a sign was given, not of the heavens, but of their spiritual myopia. (Matthew 16:1-4)

The Leaven of the Pharisees and Sadducees

As Jesus and His disciples ventured forth onto the boat that would carry them across, an air of contemplation enveloped them. The confrontation at Magdala lingered in their thoughts, intermingling with the whispers of doubt that danced in the recesses of their minds. Jesus, perceiving the tendrils of misunderstanding, cautioned them against the leaven of the

Pharisees and Sadducees. The disciples, their minds yet entangled in earthly concerns, mistook His words for a rebuke over their forgetfulness in bringing bread. But Jesus, with a patience that echoed the depths of divine understanding, guided their thoughts back to the miracles of provision, the feeding of the thousands. His words, a gentle breeze, cleared the mist of misunderstanding, revealing the true essence of the leaven of the Pharisees and Sadducees— the doctrines of deception that sought to veer the hearts of the seekers away from the path of truth. (Matthew 16:5-12)

The Revelation at Caesarea Philippi

As the sun traced its celestial arc, the entourage found itself amidst the grandeur and reverence of Caesarea Philippi. The city, nestled near a colossal rock formation, housed the ancient pagan temple of Pan. The juxtaposition of the divine and earthly resonated through the silence of the disciples as they tread along the city streets towards the outskirts, whispers of history and the divine entwined with every step.

The Question of Divinity

Upon reaching the serene outskirts, away from the hustle of religious structures, Jesus paused, His gaze sweeping over the disciples, as if peering into the corridors of their souls. The air grew still as he posed the question that reverberated through the heavens and earth, "What do people say about who I, the Son of Man, am?" The disciples, amidst the whispering winds, recounted the tales heard among the populace, of prophets reincarnated and spiritual figures reborn. Jesus listened, His eyes the calm in the storm of doubts that brewed. (Matthew 16:13-14)

The Confession

Then, shifting His gaze towards the endless sky, He brought forth another question, one that dug deeper, beyond the superficial, striking at the core of belief, "But who do you say that I am?" It was Simon Peter, his heart aflame with the truth that transcended earthly realms, who stepped forward. His voice, albeit quivering with the magnitude of revelation, resonated through the quietude as he professed, "You are the Christ, the Son of the living God." The truth, unshielded and untainted, echoed through the heartbeats of time. (Matthew 16:15-16)

The Divine Acknowledgment

Jesus, His countenance radiant with a divine glow, acknowledged Simon Peter's revelation. The words that flowed were not of this world, but a benediction from the realms above, "Blessed are you, Simon Barjona, for it is not flesh and blood that has revealed this to you, but my Father in heaven." The skies above seemed to reverberate with a divine affirmation as Jesus continued, elaborating on the essence of Peter's new identity and the establishment of His ecclesia against which the gates of hell shall not prevail. The skies whispered the divine decree, Peter's newfound mantle carried on the wings of eternity, the keys of the kingdom bestowed. (Matthew 16:17-19)

The Charge of Silence

Yet, amidst the celestial proclamation, a charge of silence was bestowed upon the disciples. The time for the revelation of the Messiah to the masses was not nigh. The journey towards the ultimate truth was yet laden with trials, confrontations, and the cross that awaited. With a gentle, yet firm admonition, Jesus urged them to withhold the revelation, a divine narrative yet to unfold in the fullness of time. (Matthew 16:20)

Foretelling The Inevitable

As the skies painted hues of forethought, the journey ushered them into realms of hard truths and divine destinies. The path they tread, though carved by celestial hands, was strewn with earthly trials and heavenly resolves.

With the breeze carrying whispers of the ancient prophecies, Jesus, amidst a solemn silence, began to unfold the narrative of what awaited Him in the city of prophets, Jerusalem. His words, etched with the burden of destiny, revealed the betrayal, suffering, and the crucifixion that awaited. Each word, though spoken with a calm resolve, carried a tempest of reality that threatened to shatter the tranquility of their hearts. (Matthew 16:21)

The earthly tremor resonated through Peter as he, seized by a blend of despair and denial, took Jesus aside. His words, wrought from the forges of love and fear, sought to rebuke the narrative of suffering. "Far be it from you, Lord; this shall not happen to you." he asserted, his voice a plea echoing the sentiments of mortal hearts yet to grasp the magnitude of divine purpose. (Matthew 16:22)

But the response from Jesus bore the weight of heavens, stern and laden with eternal significance, "Get behind me, Satan! You are a stumbling block to me, for you do not have in mind the concerns of God, but merely human concerns." It was a piercing exhortation, not just to Peter but to the realms of earthly thought that sought to divert the course of divine destiny. His eyes, deep wells of celestial wisdom, bore into the depths of their understanding, unraveling the dichotomy of divine and human wills. (Matthew 16:23)

The Call to Self-denial

Amidst the mantle of solemnity that descended, Jesus unfolded the ethos of discipleship, a calling to self-denial and the embrace of the cross. His voice, steady and unyielding, traversed the realms of earthly apprehensions, instilling the essence of losing one's life to find it in the enclaves of eternity. The eternal scales of gain and loss were laid bare, as the transient nature of earthly possessions contrasted against the enduring essence of divine fulfillment. (Matthew 16:24-26)

The Promise of the Son of Man

As the horizon bore witness, Jesus elucidated the cosmic narrative, of the Son of Man coming in His glory, accompanied by the celestial hosts to recompense each soul according to their deeds. The depiction, grand and awe-inspiring, struck a chord of reverence and anticipation, rendering a glimpse of the eschatological horizon, where justice and glory prevail under the sovereign reign of the Eternal One. (Matthew 16:27)

The Glimpse of the Kingdom

With a gentle yet profound assurance, Jesus voiced the presence of some among them who shall not taste of death till they witness the Son of Man's kingdom. The promise, enigmatic yet filled with hope, sowed seeds of divine expectancy, a foretaste of the celestial mystery that awaited unveiling in the corridors of time. (Matthew 16:28)

The unfolding narrative, a blend of earthly trials and heavenly promises, etched a deeper imprint of the Messiah's path and the journey of discipleship that beckoned each heart, under the watchful gaze of the eternal stars.

Chapter 17

The Mount of Enlightenment

The Veil Between Ages: Preceding the Mount of Revelation

The sun had dipped below the horizon, leaving behind a world cloaked in a delicate twilight. The mellowness of dusk held the promise of a profound tomorrow, one that would further unravel the majestic tapestry of the divine narrative. The disciples, with hearts filled with a blend of awe and intrigue, contemplated the unfolding revelations of their journey. The face of the Messiah, bathed in the gentle rays of the moon, held a quiet resolve as He contemplated the climb that awaited at dawn.

The night sky, strewn with stars, whispered tales of ancient prophecies, the air seemed to hold its breath in anticipation of the day that beckoned. As the disciples reclined on the cool, earthy ground, the silence of the night was their companion, a soothing balm to their stirred souls. They were on the cusp of further unveiling of heavenly mysteries, a step closer to understanding the ethereal essence of the kingdom that Jesus, the envoy of the Eternal One, ceaselessly spoke of.

The Transcendental Ascent

With the first light, the silhouettes of Jesus and his chosen three — Peter, James, and John — could be seen ascending the slopes of a hallowed mount. The terrain was rugged, but their spirits soared with a blend of anticipation and reverence as they climbed higher, the world below gradually distancing. Each step was a

step into the realms of the unknown, a journey closer to the divine essence. (Matthew 17:1)

Atop the mountain, a silence profound than ever enveloped them, and then the extraordinary unfolded. Jesus transfigured before their eyes, His face shone like the sun, his clothes became white as light. It was a spectacle of divine radiance, a window to the heavenly realm opened, the veil between earthly and divine seemed to have thinned. (Matthew 17:2)

The thin veil revealed the figures of Moses and Elijah, engaging in a heavenly dialogue with Jesus. The disciples stood at the crossroads of time, the mosaic of history and prophecy converging at this transcendental summit. (Matthew 17:3)

Overwhelmed, Peter, with a heart brimming with reverence, voiced the desire to build three tabernacles for Jesus, Moses, and Elijah. His voice quivered with the profound impact of the divine revelation, a humble attempt to honor the celestial encounter. (Matthew 17:4)

Before the words had fully escaped Peter's lips, a cloud of glory enveloped them, and a voice, the voice of the I AM resonated through the heavens and earth, affirming Jesus as His beloved Son and urging the disciples to heed Him. It was an affirmation from the very essence of creation, a divine endorsement reverberating through the annals of time. (Matthew 17:5)

The voice left the disciples face down on the ground, trembling with fear yet bathed in a reverential awe. The touch of Jesus, gentle and reassuring, urged them to arise. As they lifted their faces, the vision had ceased, leaving behind a reality that was at once both astonishing and comforting. The journey back down the mountain held a contemplative silence, the divine echo resonating within their hearts. (Matthew 17:6-9)

The Descent into Daily Realms

As they descended from the mount of revelation, questions bloomed in the hearts of the disciples, who sought understanding from Jesus regarding the coming of Elijah. Jesus, embodying the patience of the Eternal One, explained the fulfillment of prophecy through John the Baptist, his words painting a picture of a world where ancient predictions intertwine with the present, revealing the meticulously crafted divine narrative. (Matthew 17:10-13)

The Cry for Healing

As they reached the base, a crowd had gathered, their faces reflecting a mix of hope and despair. Amid them, a man knelt before Jesus, his eyes brimming with tears as he pled for his son tormented by a ruthless demon. His faith had brought him here, yet his journey was fraught with trials, as the disciples had failed to cast the vile spirit out. (Matthew 17:14-16)

Jesus' words cut through the air, his disappointment in the faithlessness around him echoed in the hearts of the disciples. The crowd around felt the weight of His words, a call to awaken from the slumber of doubt. As Jesus commanded the demon to flee, it obeyed, leaving the child restored, the awe-inspiring power of faith demonstrated for all to witness. The undercurrent of divine authority in His voice reverberated through the minds of those present, drawing them closer to the reality of the Kingdom of the Eternal One. (Matthew 17:17-18)

In the quiet space away from the crowd, the disciples, with furrowed brows, sought clarity on their inability to heal the boy. Jesus revealed the essence of faith, a force powerful enough to move mountains, yet delicate like a mustard seed. It was a lesson in the potential of unwavering faith, a glimpse into the boundless possibilities awaiting those who dare to believe beyond the seen. (Matthew 17:19-21)

Foretelling The Bitter Cup

As they traversed through the region of Galilee, Jesus' words cast a shadow of solemnity, foretelling his betrayal and death. It was a somber revelation, a bitter truth the disciples struggled to comprehend. Yet within the dark clouds of the foretold, the silver lining of resurrection shone, albeit faintly. The disciples' hearts were heavy, the impending reality of the prophecy casting a long, cold shadow over the camaraderie. (Matthew 17:22-23)

The Tribute Money

Arriving in Capernaum, the mundane duty of paying the temple tax brought them back to earthly obligations from the heavenly revelations. When questioned about the tribute, Jesus, with a hint of celestial irony, unfolded a lesson on the children of the kingdom. However, to avoid offense, a miracle unfolded with a fish bearing a coin in its mouth, enough to pay the tax for Jesus and Peter. It was a gentle brush of divine over the mundane, a whisper of the Eternal One's sovereign orchestration over both heaven and earth. (Matthew 17:24-27)

Each descent from heavenly revelations into the daily trials and chores bore with it the essence of eternal wisdom, the earthly journey intertwined with divine revelations, a path leading towards the ultimate fulfillment of the celestial narrative.

Chapter 18

Through Innocent Eyes

The Echo of Divinity in Daily Drudgery

After the celestial revelations at the luminous summit, and the small but profound teachings amid mundane matters of tribute, Jesus and His disciples continue on their divine mission. The growing throng of followers are an eclectic assembly, yearning for a piece of the divine wisdom Jesus imparts. The skies seemed to reverberate with an ancient prophecy as the group journeyed towards yet more lessons that would challenge the mundane realm with the divine truth. The air was thick with anticipation, and the rising sun cast a long shadow as they moved into the heart of Judea, where the Master was to unveil the mysteries of greatness in the Kingdom of Heaven.

Kingdom's Kernel: A Lesson in Humility

As the dusty trails of Judea settled under the weary feet of the disciples, a simmering impatience bubbled within their souls. The promised glory of the Kingdom, a topic that was often veiled in the poetic wisdom of Jesus, had kindled a flame of worldly desire amongst them. They pictured grand halls and magnificent thrones, yet the mystique of Heavenly greatness lingered like a tantalizing mirage before their hopeful eyes.

The disciples gathered around their Master under the humble shade of an old olive tree. Its gnarly branches seemed to whisper ancient secrets to those who would listen. It was under this ancient witness, the disciples with a blend of reverence and restless ambition, posed a question to Jesus. Their eyes, gleaming with a human thirst for rank and reverence, sought to unveil the criteria of greatness within the sacred realm of the Eternal One.

Jesus, with an understanding smile that seemed to traverse the chasm between the earthly and divine, scanned the earnest faces around Him. His gaze then found a child, playing in the dirt nearby with a simple piece of twig. With a tender beckoning, He called the child into their midst. The child, with an innocent smile, ambled over and stood among these seekers of truth, his simple garb a stark contrast to the serious expressions that encircled him.

Jesus, with a grace that seemed to flow from the eternal rivers of Heaven, knelt before the child, elevating the child's innocence above the restless intellect of the grown minds around. His voice, soft yet laden with a profound simplicity, explained, "Truly I tell you, unless you change and become like little children, you will never enter the Kingdom of Heaven.

Whoever humbles themselves like this little child is the greatest in the Kingdom of Heaven." (Matthew 18:3-4)

His words flowed through the air, each syllable shimmering with a divine light that seemed to pierce through the veils of worldly ambition, unveiling the heart of humility. This, Jesus revealed, was the cornerstone for those yearning to tread the path of righteousness, to transcend the earthly desire for greatness and to truly enter the exalted halls of Heaven. The disciples, enveloped in a celestial aura of understanding, beheld the emblem of divine greatness within the simplicity and purity of a child's heart.

The raw purity and innocence of the child stood as a mirror, reflecting the divine essence devoid of worldly bindings, an essence that resonated with the whisperings of the old olive tree under which they sat. The divine narrative unfolded with a clarity as crystal as the flowing streams of Galilee, leaving the disciples in a meditative silence.

In the gentle breeze that followed, the disciples could feel the heavenly wisdom seeping into the core of their being, rekindling the ember of divine ambition that burned within, refining it from the ashes of worldly desire.

The lesson of humility was a seed sown deep within their hearts, its roots promised to bear the fruits of eternal wisdom in the chapters of divine unfoldment that lay ahead.

Thus, amidst the humble whispers of the olive leaves, Jesus imprinted a profound yet simple truth upon their hearts - the key to the Kingdom lay in the heart of humility, in returning to the purity and simplicity of a child's heart, unburdened by the complexities of worldly prestige and recognition.

The serene ambiance cradled the profound realization that reverberated through the minds and hearts of the disciples, as they sat there, under the ever-wise branches of the old olive tree, embarking on an inward journey to embody the essence of a child's humility in pursuit of the eternal truth.

Stumbling Blocks and Saving Acts

The shadows lengthened as the sun marched steadily towards the western horizon, casting a golden glow on the olive leaves above. The disciples, still sitting in the calm aftermath of the lesson in humility, could feel the spiritual weight of the teachings settle upon their shoulders. The winds of change were brewing in the calm ambiance of the moment.

Jesus, noticing the earnest faces of His disciples, cradled in the early evening light, decided to delve deeper, to plant seeds of wisdom that would one day blossom into full understanding. With a tone of tender concern mixed with an unwavering firmness, Jesus unfolded the next layer of His teaching.

With a serene expression, His eyes seemed to penetrate the veil of earthly existence, reaching into the divine core of truth as He spoke. "And whoever welcomes one such child in my name welcomes me. But if anyone causes one of these little ones who believe in me to stumble, it would be better for them to have a large millstone hung around their neck and to be drowned in the depths of the sea." (Matthew 18:5-6)

The words echoed through the still air, reverberating within the hearts of the disciples. The gravity of causing a pure-hearted one to stumble unveiled itself before them. The words, laced with divine urgency, entwined around their souls like a protective cloak. They were urged, through the visceral imagery of a millstone hung around one's neck, to grasp the eternal laws that governed not just the earthly, but the celestial realm.

The disciples could almost feel the cold weight of the millstone, the eternal admonishment encased within this stark metaphor. Jesus, with a profound depth of love for His disciples, and through them, for all of mankind, wished to sow seeds of discernment, to prevent hearts from hardening, souls from faltering on the path of righteousness.

He steered their understanding further, "Woe to the world for their stumbling blocks. They are bound to happen, but how terrible it will be for the person through whom they come! So, if your hand or foot causes you to stumble, cut it off and throw it away. It's better for you to enter life with a limp or missing limb than to have both hands and feet and be thrown into the eternal fire." (Matthew 18:7-8)

The disciples listened with a riveted attention, as Jesus introduced a notion both austere and liberating. The advice of severing that which causes one to sin, though severe, was layered with an intrinsic wisdom.

It was a call to spiritual vigilance, to an unwavering allegiance to the path of righteousness even when faced with painful choices. The vivid imagery carved a deep imprint on their minds, emphasizing the necessity to maintain one's sanctity, to align with the Eternal One's divine way, even if it demanded the relinquishment of cherished yet harmful attachments.

The narrative unfolded, shedding light on the moral fabric that was to be the hallmark of the disciples' conduct, both towards themselves and the world. The panorama of divine justice and human responsibility was being painted with broad yet precise strokes by the masterful hands of Jesus.

As the discourse flowed, the disciples found themselves riding waves of enlightenment, each word from Jesus creating ripples through the lake of their understanding, expanding the horizons of their spiritual contemplation.

The calm assurance in Jesus' voice, the eternal wisdom in His words, enkindled a solemn yet empowering fire within the disciples. They were being guided, molded, and fortified for the divine journey that lay ahead, where each step was to be taken with a blend of love, wisdom, and unyielding devotion to the Eternal One's path.

And as the sky painted shades of dusk upon the canvas of the world, Jesus' teachings illuminated the dark corners of misunderstanding, gifting the disciples a torch of divine knowledge to carry through the impending trials of faith that awaited them.

The Shepherd's Heart: A Tale of The Ninety-Nine

As the day gradually melded into the tender arms of the evening, the disciples found themselves nestled in a realm of serenity, their hearts now finely tuned to the divine frequencies of Jesus' wisdom. The modest abode they occupied seemed to transcend the earthly bounds, morphing into a sanctum of celestial insight.

Jesus, with a countenance bathed in a gentle glow of the fading daylight, let his gaze wander into the distance, as if traversing the vast expanse of human existence. His voice, a melodious blend of grace and strength, began to weave the next tapestry of wisdom.

"Take heed that ye despise not one of these little ones; for I say unto you, That in heaven their angels do always behold the face of my Father which is in heaven." (Matthew 18:10)

The disciples, entranced, found themselves wandering in the lush, rolling meadows of Jesus' parable.

A serene landscape, enlivened by the lilting notes of His voice, spread before their minds' eye.

"The Son of Man has come to save the lost," Jesus continued, "What do you think? If a man has a hundred sheep, and one of them goes astray, won't he leave the ninety-nine and go into the mountains to seek the one that has gone astray?" (Matthew 18:11-12)

Each word painted strokes of divine love and relentless pursuit on the canvas of their hearts. The image of a diligent shepherd, driven by an unyielding love, leaving behind the ninety-nine to seek the one lost sheep, resonated profoundly within the quiet chamber.

The suspense of the narrative hung in the room like a gentle mist as Jesus paused. The disciples could feel the cold mountain breeze, hear the rustle of leaves under the shepherd's weary yet determined steps as he ventured into the wild terrain, the darkness of night posing no deterrence to his undying resolve.

"And if he happens to find it, I tell you, he rejoices more over that one sheep than over the ninety-nine that didn't go astray." (Matthew 18:13)

A sigh of relief, accompanied by a heartfelt joy, enveloped the room as Jesus revealed the shepherd's joy upon finding the lost sheep. It was a glimpse into the heart of the Eternal One – a heart that celebrates the return of the lost, a heart that harbors an ocean of love for each soul, regardless of their wanderings.

The room became a sanctuary where the fragrance of divine love wafted through, knitting hearts together in a tapestry of divine revelation.

"Similarly, it is not the desire of your Father in heaven that even one of these little ones should be lost." (Matthew 18:14)

The echoes of God's undying love and unyielding pursuit resonated in every heart, imprinting upon them a lesson of love, of value, and of the boundless compassion that the Eternal One harbors for each soul.

The disciples, bathed in the tender rays of the evening sun, found themselves immersed in a boundless sea of love that transcended the earthly understanding of worth and loyalty. The Shepherd's tale wasn't merely a story. It was a bridge to the heart of the Eternal One, a beckoning for them to emulate this boundless love in their journey, a love that saw no bounds, that knew no limits, a love that mirrored the heart of the divine Shepherd – the heart of the Eternal One.

As night gently unfurled its veil over the day, the hearts in the room glowed with a celestial flame, the echoes of the Shepherd's heart humming in their souls as they tread further into the realms of divine understanding.

Bridging Discord:
The Path of Reconciliation

As the night deepened its embrace, the celestial dance of the stars above mirrored the divine dance of wisdom unfolding in the modest dwelling below. The humble abode, where the disciples huddled around Jesus, resonated with the rhythms of heavenly truths. The outside world seemed to fade, its incessant clamor drowned in the profound silence that heralded the next wave of divine insight.

Jesus, with a countenance reflecting the peace of the heavenly realms, navigated their consciousness towards the tempestuous seas of human discord. His eyes, those deep pools of serenity, seemed to pierce through the veil of earthly entanglements, laying bare the roots of discord that often threatened the harmony of existence.

"Furthermore, if your brother wrongs you, go and speak to him privately, just the two of you. If he listens to you, you have won back your brother." (Matthew 18:15)

The simplicity yet profound wisdom of His counsel resonated through the silence. It was a beacon of light amidst the murky clouds of misunderstanding and resentment. The pathway to reconciliation He was unveiling was like a sacred bridge, capable of spanning the chasms of discord that often yawned between souls.

"But if he refuses to listen, then bring one or two others with you, so that by the testimony of two or three witnesses, every matter may be established." (Matthew 18:16)

The disciples could almost visualize the steps of this bridge, each stone laid with love, patience, and a yearning for harmony. It was not just a lesson in con-

flict resolution, but an initiation into a higher way of being, where love and understanding triumphed over ego and discord.

"If he still refuses to listen, then bring the matter before the assembly. And if he disregards the assembly's decision, treat him as you would a stranger or a tax collector." (Matthew 18:17)

His words, filled with the essence of divine love and practical wisdom, contained the blueprint for harmonious existence. A way to echo the celestial harmony amidst the cacophony of earthly existence.

"I tell you the truth, whatever you bind on earth will be bound in heaven, and whatever you loose on earth will be loosed in heaven." (Matthew 18:18)

As Jesus elaborated on the binding and loosing, the disciples were drawn deeper into the mysteries of divine justice and mercy, intertwined with the earthly endeavors of reconciliation.

"Once more I tell you, if two of you on earth agree about anything you ask for, it will be done for you by my Father in heaven. For where two or three gather in my name, I am there among them." (Matthew 18:19-20)

The atmosphere vibrated with the sacredness of unity, the power of agreement, and the presence of the divine amidst the endeavor of souls striving for harmony. It was a glimpse into the celestial fellowship, an invitation to bring forth heaven on earth through the portals of love, understanding, and reconciliation.

As the profound reverberations of His teachings nestled in their hearts, the disciples found themselves armed with a divine blueprint. A blueprint that beckoned them to rise above the ephemeral discord, to build bridges of love amidst the storms of misunderstandings, to echo the celestial harmony in the symphony of earthly existence.

The soft glow of the lingering dusk tenderly kissed the humble abode as the disciples nestled into a space of deeper contemplation, the embers of divine wisdom glowing warmly in the hearth of their souls.

The Abundance of Forgiveness Expanded

The gentle canopy of the night stretched far and wide, as the flickering flames of the solitary lamp cast long shadows upon the humble dwelling. The atmosphere was imbued with a profound quietude, a sacred pause, as if the Universe itself leaned in to partake in the enigmatic unraveling of divine mysteries

by Jesus. As the solemn silence settled amongst the disciples, it was Peter, ever ardent in his quest for understanding, who disrupted the calm with a question that bore the weight of earthly dilemmas.

"Lord, how many times should I forgive my brother when he sins against me? Seven times?" (Matthew 18:21)

His voice carried the earnest strivings of humanity in understanding the complex tapestry of forgiveness. The question hung in the solemn stillness, its ripples stirring the tranquility that enshrouded the room.

Jesus, the tranquil shepherd of their souls, met Peter's inquiry with a gaze that seemed to span the depths of eternity. His response bore the essence of boundless mercy, echoing through the corridors of time and space.

"I don't say to you, seven times, but rather, seventy times seven." (Matthew 18:22)

The room seemed to reverberate with the unutterable profundity of His words. They were invited into a realm where forgiveness wasn't merely an act but a divine state of being, an infinite expression of God's mercy.

With a cadence of a gentle stream flowing over soft pebbles, Jesus began narrating a tale that was to etch the eternal principles of forgiveness onto the hearts of his listeners. It was the tale of a king, whose mercy resembled the boundless expanse of the heavens, and a servant, whose heart harbored the harsh cliffs of mercilessness.

"Thus, the Kingdom of Heaven is similar to a king who decided to settle accounts with his servants." (Matthew 18:23)

As Jesus spun the narrative, the modest room transcended the earthly confines, morphing into a grand royal court where the interplay of mercy and justice unfolded before the eyes of the disciples.

The narrative wove through the heart-wrenching plea of the servant, the boundless mercy of the king, and the cruel irony of the servant's subsequent mercilessness toward his fellow servant. Each word, each scene unfurled layers of divine wisdom, teaching the timeless lesson of grace, mercy, and the heavenly mandate of forgiveness.

"But that very servant went outside and encountered one of his fellow servants who owed him a hundred pence. He seized him and choked him, demanding, 'Pay me what you owe!'" (Matthew 18:28)

The parable reached its crescendo with the king's wrath upon the unforgiving servant, a mirror reflecting the divine equilibrium of justice and mercy.

"In the same way, my Heavenly Father will treat you unless you truly forgive each other from the depths of your hearts." (Matthew 18:35)

As Jesus' words settled in the hushed room, the parable left an indelible mark on the disciples' hearts. The narrative dissolved, leaving behind a vast expanse of contemplation where the disciples could glimpse the heart of the Eternal One - boundless in mercy, steadfast in justice.

The divine narrative had transported them beyond the earthly dimensions, into the heart of eternal truths. The night seemed to bow in reverence to the divine unfolding, as the disciples nestled into a profound silence, each heart nursing the infinite seeds of forgiveness sown by the gentle words of the Master. They were left in the gentle embrace of the night, each heart echoing with the divine melody of mercy and forgiveness.

Chapter 19

The Heart of the Covenant

A Light Unto the Path

As dawn cast a soft glow on the horizon, the city of Jerusalem shimmered in the early light, awaiting the arrival of a teacher who held the keys to the mysteries of heaven. Jesus, with his disciples, prepared to embark on yet another day filled with inquiries, enlightenment, and challenges. As they approached the city, the skies opened up in a brilliant dance of colors, signifying a day that would be etched in the hearts of many. The morning air carried whispers of anticipation as the crowd gathered, yearning for the eternal wisdom that was to flow from the lips of Jesus.

The Sanctity of Marriage

Upon the arrival of Jesus and His disciples in the regions of Judaea beyond Jordan, a place where the Jordan river flowed like a ribbon of life through the ancient landscapes, the people's hearts throbbed with anticipation. The sun cast a gentle glow on the faces of the multitude that had assembled, their eyes reflecting the yearning for divine wisdom. The aura of Jesus carried the calmness of eternity, His presence a gentle river that soothed the perturbed hearts in a turbulent world. With the heavens witnessing below, Jesus stood amidst the gathering as the embodiment of love and divine law.

The Pharisees, ever eager to ensnare Jesus in a web of words, approached with a question that danced on the edge of legality and divine decree. "Is it lawful," they inquired, a guise of innocence masking the snare in their words, "for a man to divorce his wife for any reason." (Matthew 19:3) The crowd hushed as the inquiry echoed through the still air, awaiting the answer that would flow from the lips of Jesus.

Jesus, His eyes reflecting the depths of heavenly wisdom, delved into the annals of Creation. He reminded them of the divine sketch where 'Male and Female' were drawn together in an eternal bond, the narrative of Genesis unfurling before their eyes. "Have ye not read," He said with an aura of gentle rebuke, "that He which made them at the beginning made them male and female,." (Matthew 19:4) The image of Adam and Eve, bound by love in the pristine Garden of Eden, floated across the minds of the assembled. The divine intent behind the sacred institution of marriage was being unveiled.

As the murmurs of realization fluttered through the crowd, Jesus continued, addressing the hardness of hearts that sought to sever what the Eternal One had bound together. (Matthew 19:8) He delved into the legality of divorce, His words shedding light on the heart of God regarding the permanence of marital bonds.

Then came a discourse that peeled layers off the veils that clouded earthly understanding. Jesus spoke of eunuchs, those who chose a life of celibacy for the Kingdom of Heaven's sake, their path, a reflection of sublime sacrifices and heavenly allegiance. (Matthew 19:12) His words carried the essence of divine ordinances, transcending human traditions, and earthly desires, guiding the souls unto paths of righteousness.

The teaching left the multitude in contemplation, the Pharisees in thought, and the disciples in deeper reverence for the eternal principles that governed the heavens and the earth. The sun set with a promise of a new dawn of understanding as the words of Jesus resonated through the ancient landscapes, echoing within the chambers of the heart, guiding the seekers onto paths of eternal truth.

The Kingdom's Heirs:
Blessing the Little Ones

As the sun cast long shadows across the land, painting the ancient terrain with shades of gold and crimson, a soft murmur of wonder continued to ripple through the gathered souls. The teachings on marriage and celibacy had planted seeds of divine truth, prompting inward reflection among the seekers and Pharisees alike. Yet, the day was far from over, and the thirst for wisdom was a river that flowed unceasingly.

Soon, the scene morphed into a tableau of innocence and divine tenderness. From the crowd emerged parents, their eyes reflecting the boundless hopes and dreams nestled within their hearts. In their arms and by their hands, they brought their children, the apples of their eyes, to Jesus. They desired the touch of blessings, a divine embrace that would shield these tender buds from the world's storms and thorns. The scene was a living portrait of hope and love intertwined, waiting for the gentle touch of the divine.

Yet, the disciples, perhaps weary from the day or lost in the maze of doctrines and crowd control, sought to restrain them. The voices of admonition, born out of concern or misunderstanding, attempted to form a barrier between Jesus and the children. But Jesus, His eyes radiating the warmth of a thousand suns, beheld the scene with a different vision.

"Allow the little children to come to me," He spoke gently yet with unwavering resolve, "and do not hinder them, for the Kingdom of Heaven belongs to such as these." (Matthew 19:14) With these words, a divine mystery was unveiled. The veil lifted, revealing the kingdom's keys held within the grasp of purity, innocence, and unyielding trust, qualities mirrored in the eyes of the children now drawing near to Jesus.

He stretched forth His hands, and as they descended upon the soft curls and tender crowns, blessings flowed like rivers of living water. Each touch was a shower of divine love, each blessing a shield of eternal protection, each smile a glimpse into the heavenly realms. The disciples watched, their hearts being schooled in the divine curriculum of humility and trust.

The parents, with tears of joy and gratitude glistening in their eyes, beheld the scene of divine love encircling their precious ones. The purity and simplicity encapsulated in this moment were like keys unlocking deeper realms of understanding.

The sky now bathed in the soft hues of dusk bore witness to the unfolding scene. The sun took a bow, leaving behind a horizon aglow with celestial fire as Jesus, with a heart that embraced the little and the lost, unfolded the mysteries of the Kingdom. The essence of this divine act danced upon the twilight breeze, whispering the ancient truth – in humility and purity, the gates of heaven swing open.

The Rich Young Man's Quest

Amid the dissolving crowd emerged a figure, his gait steady yet laden with the subtle tremors of an earnest seeking. He was a young man, his countenance reflecting the opulence of his earthly stature, yet his eyes were wells of earnest seeking, probing the veils between the mundane and the mystic. Approaching Jesus, he knelt with a reverence that blended humility with desperation. His voice trembled as he posed the question that perhaps echoed the collective human strife, "Good Master, what good thing shall I do, that I may have eternal life?" (Matthew 19:16)

Jesus, with a gaze that pierced through the veils of human pretensions and reached the core of sincere seeking, replied, "Why do you call me good?" he asked. "There is only One who is truly good—God. If you want to enter life, keep the commandments." (Matthew 19:17) It was a response that bore the essence of divine laws, guiding the young man to the foundational stones of righteousness.

The young man, not deterred but spurred by Jesus's words, inquired further, "Which?" Jesus then recited the commandments, the divine codes engraved in the annals of the holy scriptures, the age-old lanterns illuminating the path of righteousness. (Matthew 19:18-19)

With a quiver of hope, the young man responded, "I have kept all these commandments, what else do I lack?" (Matthew 19:20) His eyes sparkled with the desire for the unseen, for the eternal realms that beckoned the pure at heart.

Jesus beheld him with a love profound, a love that discerned the thistles on the path of the earnest seeker. His next words were a divine invitation and a challenge intertwined, "If you wish to be truly complete, sell your possessions, give to those in need, and you will amass heavenly treasure. Then, come and walk this path with me" (Matthew 19:21) It was a call to transcend the tangible, to let go of the worldly anchors, to embrace the path of divine surrender.

But as the words cascaded over the young man's spirit, a tempest brewed in his heart. The battle between the earthly and the divine, the ephemeral and the eternal raged with a ferocity that left him pale. The reality of the divine directive, the sacrificial leap into the unknown, weighed heavily upon his soul. With a heart now shrouded in sorrow, he withdrew from the divine presence, for he had many possessions, earthly treasures that chained him to the transient shores. (Matthew 19:22)

The silence that ensued was a silent sermon, a mirror reflecting the age-old human plight - the struggle between the ephemeral comforts and the call of eternal bliss.

The Eye of a Needle: Path of The Wealthy

As the silhouette of the wealthy young man blurred into the horizon, a profound lesson lingered in the hearts of the disciples. The scene was a parable unfolding in real-time, shedding light on the intricate tapestry of earthly desires and heavenly pursuits. Jesus, seizing this moment of potent revelation, turned to his disciples and spoke words that would reverberate through the chambers of their understanding, "Truly I tell you, it is difficult for a wealthy person to enter the Kingdom of Heaven" (Matthew 19:23).

The disciples, a motley crew of humble backgrounds, were struck by the stark imagery Jesus then portrayed, "Again I say unto you, It is easier for a camel to go through the eye of a needle, than for a

rich man to enter into the Kingdom of God."
(Matthew 19:24) The metaphor was profound, painting
a vivid picture of the gargantuan challenge faced by
those shackled by worldly wealth in navigating the
narrow paths leading to the divine dominion. It was a
statement that didn't just echo amidst the ancient
stones but pierced through the veil of material illu-
sions, reaching the core of divine truth.

Jesus' words stirred a sea of contemplation among
the disciples. They were individuals who had left behind the meager or moderate possessions they had to
follow the path laid out by Jesus. The rich young
man's inability to do the same raised a tempest of
wonder and concern among them. The path they
tread was laden with trials, yet it was also the road to
eternal glory. This dichotomy brewed a storm of

questions, among which emerged a desperate plea for understanding, "Who then can be saved?" (Matthew 19:25)

With a compassionate gaze, Jesus beheld their troubled hearts. His reply was a balm to the furrows of worry etched on their faces. "With men this is impossible; but with God all things are possible." (Matthew 19:26) These words were a stream of celestial hope flowing through the arid lands of human limitation. They spoke of a divine intervention that could turn the tides, that could guide the lost and the shackled towards the realms of divine salvation.

The discourse etched the essence of divine possibility into the hearts of disciples, a lesson in the inexhaustible grace of the Eternal One which could guide even the most entangled hearts towards the serenity of His boundless Kingdom.

The Disciples' Inheritance

The contemplative silence that draped around the disciples was pierced by Peter's earnest inquiry. He, like others, had forsaken familiar shores, embarking on a voyage into the divine mysteries under the wing of Jesus. A blend of curiosity and hope twinkled in his eyes as he posed a question that resonated the collec-

tive heartbeat of the disciples, "Look, we have left everything to follow you. What then will there be for us?" (Matthew 19:27) Peter's voice carried the weight of sacrifices made, families left behind, and former lives relinquished in pursuit of a higher calling.

Jesus, with an expression of deep understanding and a love that enveloped them in warmth, directed their gaze beyond the temporal veil into the eternal landscapes. He spoke of a time of celestial reckoning, where the Son of Man shall sit in the throne of his glory, and the disciples too, shall sit upon twelve thrones, judging the twelve tribes of Israel. (Matthew 19:28) It was a glimpse into a grandiose vista where divine justice and love reigned supreme, a promise of an inheritance that transcended earthly comprehension.

The words of Jesus carried them further into the mystic realms of divine reciprocity, "And everyone who has left houses or brothers or sisters or father or mother or children or fields for my sake will receive a hundred times as much and will inherit eternal life." (Matthew 19:29) These were words that seeded eternal hope in the hearts that had chosen the path of divine discipleship, reassuring them of a magnificent return for their earthly renunciations. It was a revelation that every sacrifice made in His name was a step closer to eternal glory, each relinquishment a cultivation of celestial riches.

But amidst this promise of divine reward, Jesus interwove a timeless principle that resonated through the dimensions of earthly and heavenly existence, "But many that are first shall be last; and the last shall be first." (Matthew 19:30) This divine paradox was a mirror reflecting the heart of God's kingdom, a realm where the humble are exalted, and the exalted are humbled. It was a final stroke in the divine picture painted by Jesus, depicting the great equalization in the heart of the Eternal One, where every soul was precious, and every sacrifice held invaluable.

CHAPTER 20

THE LAST, THE FIRST

Dawning Hues of Divine Discourse

As the disciples traversed the beaten paths of Judea with Jesus, the essence of the previous discourses still lingered, weaving a tapestry of anticipation for the celestial wisdom yet to be unveiled. The sun cast a gentle glow, heralding the dawn of fresh teachings as they neared Jerusalem. Amid the quiet rustle of morning breeze, the disciples gathered around Jesus, their hearts aflutter with the promise of divine narratives awaiting to unravel the profound mysteries of the Kingdom of Heaven. As the veil of earthly comprehension gently lifted, they stood on the brink of a deeper understanding, ready to delve into the realms of divine equity that the Messiah was about to elucidate through a parable.

The Parable of the Workers in the Vineyard

In a tranquil morning, as the rays of dawn painted the skies with hues of hope, Jesus found himself amidst a gathering of souls yearning for wisdom. Seated on a gentle hillock, His serene countenance drew the masses closer as they hung onto every word that flowed from His lips. It was a moment of divine dissemination where hearts found resonance in His teachings. With a view of the verdant fields stretching out in the distance, Jesus began to unfurl the mysteries of the Kingdom of Heav-

en, employing the humble yet profound analogy of a vineyard.

"The Kingdom of Heaven," Jesus began, his voice casting a tranquil spell over the eager crowd, "is like unto a man that is a householder, which went out early in the morning to hire laborers into his vineyard." (Matthew 20:1)

He elucidated, transporting them to a quaint, picturesque setting of a vineyard where the morning mist met the first rays of the sun. The landowner, a kind-hearted man of virtue, steps into the early market hustle to hire workers promising a fair wage of a denarius for their toil. The first rays of hope in the laborer's eyes reflected the warmth of dawn as they embarked on the day's endeavor. (Matthew 20:2)

As Jesus continued, the crowd could envision the scene transitioning with the sun climbing higher in the sky. "And he went out about the third hour, and saw others standing idle in the marketplace, And said unto them; Go ye also into the vineyard, and whatsoever is right I will give you. And they went their way." Jesus said, revealing the boundless compassion of the houscholder towards the idle workers as they too find a purpose in the fertile fields of the vineyard. (Matthew 20:3-4)

Jesus further unraveled the tale as the day unfolded in the parable, the landowner's recurring visits to the marketplace at the sixth and the ninth hours showcased a relentless quest to ensure every willing soul found work and sustenance. The divine narrative showcased a compassionate providence encompassing every soul, irrespective of the hour. (Matthew 20:5-7)

As dusk cast a tranquil veil on the vineyard, Jesus led the listeners to the moment of reckoning. The time of wage distribution was a profound metaphor for divine grace and justice. The householder's instruction to his steward to begin with the last reflected the celestial principle of divine generosity. The narrative escalated with the reactions of the workers who toiled since dawn, their hearts fluttering with the expectation of more, only to be met with a gentle reprimand from the householder. Jesus echoed the landowner's profound words, "Friend, I am not being unfair to you. Didn't you agree to work for a denarius? Take your pay and go. I want to give the one who was hired last the same as I gave you." (Matthew 20:13-14)

With the final discourse, Jesus crystallized the profound essence of God's kingdom, "So the last shall be first, and the first last: for many be called, but few chosen." The crowd was swept into a profound silence as they delved into the essence of the tale. The parable served as a mirror reflecting the divine principles of equality, justice, and God's boundless grace, painting a vivid picture of the Kingdom of Heaven within the earthly framework of a vineyard. (Matthew 20:16)

Jesus Foretells His Death and Resurrection

As the sun embarked on its descent, casting long shadows on the dusty path, a somber mood veiled the disciples. They had traversed through towns, preaching the Kingdom, healing the sick, and drawing countless to the beacon of hope that was Jesus. Yet, the road they trod was leading them towards Jerusalem, a city echoing with the chants of tradition and the rustle of ancient prophecies. There was a

palpable tension in the air, a chilling foreshadowing that crept into the hearts of the disciples as they clustered around Jesus, who walked with a solemn yet resolute stride.

Jesus, sensing the unease among his disciples, decided it was time to unveil the mysteries that lay ahead. They found respite under the shade of an ancient olive tree, its gnarled branches stretching out like the hands of time. Jesus turned to them, his eyes deep pools of celestial wisdom and beckoned them closer. "Behold, we go up to Jerusalem; and the Son of Man shall be betrayed unto the chief priests and unto the scribes, and they shall condemn him to death," He said, each word dripping with a somber reality that hung heavily upon the hearts of His disciples. (Matthew 20:18)

The wind carried away the whispered fears as the disciples listened with bated breath. The landscape around seemed to hold its breath as Jesus continued, "And shall deliver him to the Gentiles to mock, and to scourge, and to crucify him…" The words reverberated through the silence, weaving a tapestry of dread intertwined with divine purpose. They couldn't fathom the gravity of what awaited their beloved Master, a fate so harsh for a heart so tender. (Matthew 20:19a)

Yet amidst the looming darkness, Jesus' voice bore a note of triumph as he continued, "...and the third day he shall rise again." The words sparked a glimmer of hope, a mystery so profound that it seemed to challenge the shackles of mortality. It was a promise of victory over the abyss, a glimmer of eternal dawn awaiting beyond the tempest. (Matthew 20:19b)

The silence that followed was a journey into the depths of faith, a mingling of fear, and hope. The disciples exchanged glances, their faces etched with the markings of contemplation. They were on the cusp of unfolding destiny, a divine plot that was set against the backdrop of earthly trials and celestial triumph. The path ahead was laden with thorns of sacrifice, yet at its end lay the rose of resurrection.

A Mother's Request and Lessons of Servitude

Under the canopy of the noonday sun, the breeze carried a hint of Jerusalem's imminence as the fellowship of disciples strolled the well-trodden paths. The anticipation of what lay ahead in the sacred city wrapped around their hearts like a vine. Amidst the disciples, the sons of Zebedee, James and John, journeyed with a quiet sense of earnestness. The narrative

of the Messiah was intricately intertwined with their own, yet the horizon of destiny was veiled in mystery.

Suddenly, the serene procession was touched by a tender urgency as the mother of James and John, with her heart brimming with maternal hope and a dash of worldly aspiration, approached Jesus. With a respectful demeanor, she knelt before the Master, the very picture of a mother's love entwined with a plea for assurance. "Master," she beseeched, "Can you allow my two sons to have the honored seats, one on your right and one on your left, in your kingdom?" (Matthew 20:21)

Jesus, with eyes that held the tranquil depth of the eternal, gazed upon the mother and her sons. He understood the maternal love that veiled a desire for a distinguished place for her sons in the unfolding divine narrative. Yet, it was a moment ripe for an invaluable lesson. Turning to James and John, He posed, "You don't really understand what you're asking for. Can you handle drinking from the same cup I'll drink from, and being baptized with the same baptism I'll experience?" Their eager affirmation echoed the stirrings of valiant but yet untested hearts. "We are able," they declared, their faces firm with resolve. (Matthew 20:22)

Jesus, in His boundless wisdom, saw beyond the veil of the earthly realm, into the crucible of divine destiny awaiting them. "You will indeed drink from my cup and be baptized with the baptism that I am baptized with," He affirmed, acknowledging the path of sacrifice and service that lay ahead for them. Yet, the seats of honor they sought were not His to grant. "To sit at my right hand and at my left is not mine to grant, but it will be given to those for whom it has been prepared by my Father." (Matthew 20:23)

The dialog did not escape the ears of the other disciples, and a wave of discontent, mixed with a touch of rivalry, stirred amongst them. Jesus perceived the ripple of discord and beckoned them unto Him. Under the warm embrace of the sunlight, His words flowed like a gentle stream, addressing not just the assembly, but the ages to come. "You know that the rulers of the Gentiles lord it over them, and their high officials exercise authority over them. Not so with you." (Matthew 20:25-26a)

His message was a call to a higher realm, a celestial hierarchy where greatness was entwined with service and humility. "Whoever wants to be great among you must be your servant, and whoever wants to be first among you must be your slave" His words soared beyond the earthly understanding of rank, into the

divine realms where love and service reigned supreme. "Just as the Son of Man did not come to be served, but to serve, and to give his life as a ransom for many." (Matthew 20:26b-28)

The veil of worldly ambition was gently lifted, revealing the pristine glory of servitude, resonating with the eternal pulse of love and sacrifice. This was the melody of the Kingdom, a tune set to the rhythm of selfless service, echoing the very heartbeat of the Eternal One.

The Healing of Two Blind Men

As the entourage approached the outskirts of Jericho, a city ripe with history, the whispers of the olden days danced through the ancient ruins and murmured through the rustling leaves. The city had witnessed the touch of the divine many a time, yet the populace awaited, with bated breath, the tales of miracles and wisdom that accompanied Jesus.

Amidst the bustling crowd, two blind men sat by the wayside, bound to the spot by the shackles of their infirmity, yet their spirits soared with the hope of divine touch. Their ears, attuned to the whispers of faith, caught the rustling of the gathering, the murmurs of Jesus' name, a name adorned with the hope of the oppressed. The rustling grew into a crescendo of murmurs, an indication of His near approach. Their hearts raced, fueled by tales of wonders they had heard; they were desperate for a miracle.

With the meek sun casting long shadows on the path, their cries cut through the casual banter of the crowd. "Have mercy on us, O Lord, thou son of David!" they cried out, their voices an echo of desperation and faith intertwining into a plea that soared through the canopy of leaves, touching the heavens. (Matthew 20:30) The crowd, a mixture of curiosity and reverence in their midst, was initially irked. Many shushed them, the word 'silence' rippling through like a harsh wind. But their cries only grew in fervency, the name of 'Son of David' resonating with the depth of Messianic hope.

Jesus halted, the whispers of divine compassion moving His heart. He called them over. Amidst the parting crowd, with hands trembling with anticipation, they approached the Master, the source of their hope. The soft, compassionate gaze of Jesus met the sightless eyes that bore years of darkness yet sparkled with the light of faith. "What do you want me to do for you?" He inquired, His voice a gentle, reassuring balm. (Matthew 20:32)

With hearts throbbing with the hope of light, they implored, "Lord, that our eyes may be opened." Their plea was simple, yet carried the depth of years of desperate prayers for mercy. (Matthew 20:33) In a moment suspended in divine compassion, Jesus, moved with pity, touched their eyes. The act was gentle, yet the heavens trembled with power as sight, like a tender dawn, broke through the darkness that had been their world. In the caress of light, they beheld the face of their Savior, the embodiment of divine love and power.

The sight of the miracle unfurled like a divine scroll, and the crowd that bore witness erupted in a symphony of praises. The atmosphere was charged with awe, the reality of the divine interwoven with the mundane. The blind men, now beholders of light, were the living testimony of the merciful touch of the

Eternal One. Their first vision was the compassionate face of Jesus, a sight engrained in their souls as they followed Him, their hearts aflame with gratitude, faith and love, singing praises unto the God of miracles. (Matthew 20:34)

The road to Jerusalem was adorned with the footprints of the divine, an invitation to the realm of faith where the I AM reigned with mercy and love.

Chapter 21

The King's Entry

The Dawning Horizon

As the first rays of the sun cast a soft glow on the modest dwelling in Bethany, the disciples of Jesus found themselves encircled in reflection. The miracles they had witnessed, the blind men now beholding the daylight, the teachings about the Kingdom of Heaven, were all swirling in a divine dance in their minds. Yet, amongst them arose a tingling anticipation, like a leaf quivering at the touch of the breeze. The path ahead was leading them to Jerusalem, the heart of prophecies and promises. The air seemed to thicken with a blend of hope and trepidation, each heart bearing its rhythm as they neared the pivotal juncture of their journey with the Lord.

Jesus, the embodiment of serenity amid the whirlpool of thoughts, sensed the burgeoning hope and the veil of uncertainties among His followers. His gaze wandered over the horizon towards Jerusalem, the city that now awaited His arrival. The disciples, catching the flicker of resolve in His eyes, felt an inexplicable meld of awe and courage knitting within their spirits. The Master had unfurled the mysteries of heaven, yet, a deeper understanding awaited them. As the horizon beckoned, the path to Jerusalem now shimmered with both the shadows of earthly trials and the foreshadow of divine fulfillment.

The Triumphant Entry

The dawn of a new day unfolded as Jesus and His disciples approached the outskirts of Jerusalem. The city, which stood as a symbol of religious tradition and hope for the Jewish people, seemed to breathe with anticipation. Jesus, knowing the importance of the journey ahead, instructed two of his disciples to venture into the village ahead and procure a donkey tied there along with a colt. The specificity of His instructions was a puzzle yet a marvel to His disciples as they set forth on the task assigned. "You will find a donkey tied, along with a colt. Untie them and bring them to me. If anyone asks why you are taking them, say, 'The Lord needs them,' and he will immediately send them." Jesus'

words carried an essence of divine certainty as they echoed in the hearts of His disciples. (Matthew 21:2-3)

As the disciples found the donkey and colt, just as Jesus had mentioned, they were reminded of a verse from the prophecies. The ancient words of Zechariah unfurled in their minds, "Tell the daughter of Zion, 'Behold, your King comes to you, meek and sitting on a donkey, even a colt, the foal of a donkey.'" The fulfillment of the prophecy stood before them, living and breathing, a weave of divine orchestration that was about to unveil itself. The disciples laid their garments upon the animals, creating a makeshift saddle, indicating honor and submission to Jesus, who humbly seated Himself upon the donkey. As He rode towards Jerusalem, the disciples were caught in a rapture of reverence and awe, as the Old Testament words found flesh and breath in their midst. (Matthew 21:4-5)

The arrival of Jesus in Jerusalem was unlike any other. The city that had witnessed the comings and goings of kings and prophets now trembled with a divine ripple. Crowds began to gather, their hearts ignited with the sparks of hope and recognition. They spread their garments on the road, while others cut branches from the trees to lay in His path, a traditional sign of homage and royalty. The cries of "Hosanna to the Son of David: Blessed is he that comes in the name of the Lord; Hosanna in the highest," resonated through the walls and valleys, announcing the entry of a King, yet not any king, the King of Peace, the fulfillment of ancient hopes. Yet, amidst the jubilations, the city was moved, and questions arose among them. "Who is this?" they inquired, the name of Jesus reverberated through the streets, intertwining with the prophecies, mysteries, and the hope for salvation. (Matthew 21:8-10)

Jesus Cleanses the Temple

As the shadows of the afternoon sun draped over Jerusalem, the atmosphere was thick with spiritual anticipation and earthly concern. The Holy Temple, the epicenter of religious life, had become a marketplace. It was here where devout hearts sought connection with the Divine, but were now met with the clinking of coins, the bickering over prices, and the cold indifference of a transactional faith. Merchants and money changers had set their stalls amid the sacred, the clattering of their commerce echoing through the chambers of worship. What was once a house of prayer, stood entangled with the desires and deceptions of earthly gain. (Matthew 21:12a)

Jesus, with an intensity in His eyes, entered the temple. His gaze swept across the courtyard, piercing through the veil of hypocrisy, reaching the heart of the temple's desecration. In a zeal propelled by divine righteousness, He overthrew the tables of the money changers, and the seats of them that sold doves. His actions were like a storm that swept through the temple, clearing away the debris of greed and dishonesty. His voice, firm yet laden with a holy sorrow, resonated through the chaos, "It is written, My house shall be called the House of Prayer; but ye have made it a den of thieves." His words were a sharp contrast to the tinkling coins, a call back to sacredness amidst the profane. His actions weren't just a cleansing, but a restoring of the divine order, a reclamation of the sacred over the worldly. (Matthew 21:12b-13)

The repercussions of Jesus' actions reverberated through the stone walls of the temple and into the hearts of those present. The religious leaders, beholding the authority and boldness of Jesus, were filled with indignation. Their positions, built upon the pedestals of religious dogma and societal prestige, trembled under the righteous zeal of Jesus. Meanwhile, the blind and the lame approached Him in the temple, and He healed them, embodying the pure essence of the temple as a place of divine connection and restoration. The marvels of His deeds and the innocence of children who cried, "Hosanna to the Son of David," were a living testament to the God He represented, further igniting the disdain of the religious leaders. The religious elite, threatened and enraged, failed to recognize the dawn of salvation unfolding before their very eyes. Yet, amid their plotting hearts, the masses saw hope, a break from religious tyranny, and a glimpse into the heart of God. (Matthew 21:14-16)

The Fig Tree Withered

The morning light was dawning, casting a golden hue over the land as Jesus made His way back to the city from Bethany. The tranquility of the morning was a stark contrast to the preceding day's events in the temple. The path was lined with trees, their branches rustling softly in the morning breeze. Among them, a solitary fig tree stood, its leaves vibrant and inviting, a symbol of potential nourishment and sustenance. But upon closer inspection, Jesus found it barren, void of the fruit it promised. A mirage of fulfillment. (Matthew 21:18-19a)

With a heavy heart, Jesus addressed the fig tree, "Let no fruit grow on you from now on, forever." The words were not just a judgment on a tree, but a poignant metaphor for Israel, especially its religious leaders who flaunted an exterior of piety but were devoid of true spiritual fruits. Just as swiftly as His words were uttered, the fig tree withered away, its leaves shriveling, its vitality gone, symbolizing the fate of fruitless lives. The disciples, witnessing this, marveled at the immediacy of its withering, exclaiming, "The fig tree withered away immediately!" (Matthew 21:19b-20)

Jesus seized this moment, turning their astonishment into a lesson on the potency of unwavering faith and the power of prayer. Looking intently at them, He declared, "If you have unwavering faith and doubt not, not only can you do what was done to the fig tree, but also you can say to this mountain, 'Be removed and thrown into the sea,' and it will happen." This was not just about moving physical mountains, but the insurmountable challenges of life, the barriers in one's spiritual journey. He further assured them,

"And anything you ask for in prayer, as long as you have faith, you will receive." A promise that anchored them to the power of faith and the limitless possibilities when one's trust is rooted in the Eternal One. (Matthew 21:21-22)

Authority Challenged

In the temple courts, as Jesus resumed teaching, the chief priests and elders approached Him, their robes swishing with an air of authority. Their faces, stern and disapproving, revealed their intentions even before they spoke. With voices dripping with condescension, they inquired, "By whose authority are you doing these things? And who gave you this authority?" Their question wasn't rooted in genuine curiosity but was a calculated challenge, an attempt to corner Jesus and undermine His influence among the masses. (Matthew 21:23)

Jesus, perceiving their motives, responded not with a direct answer but with a counter-question, turning the tables on His interrogators. "I also will ask you one thing," He began, "The baptism of John, was it from heaven or from men?" The question placed the religious leaders in a precarious position. If they acknowledged John's baptism as divine, it would raise questions about their rejection of John. But to deny its

heavenly origin would risk the ire of the crowds who revered John as a prophet. (Matthew 21:24-26)

Caught in their own snare, the leaders exchanged nervous glances, weighing their options. Finally, choosing the safer route, they replied, "We cannot tell." Jesus, asserting His wisdom over their schemes, responded, "I won't tell you by what authority I do these things either." It was a masterclass in divine wisdom, revealing the hollowness of their self-righteousness and showcasing Jesus's unparalleled authority in both word and deed. (Matthew 21:27)

Parable of the Two Sons

Amidst the tension following His encounter with the chief priests and elders, Jesus, as was His custom, delved into a parable, seeking to shed light on the hearts of those around Him. He began, "But what do you think? There was a man who had two sons." He narrated the story of a father who asked both his sons to work in his vineyard. While the first initially refused but later went, the second agreed but did not follow through with his promise. (Matthew 21:28-30)

Jesus then posed a question to His audience, challenging their preconceptions. "Which of the two did the will of his father?" The religious leaders, drawn

into the simplicity of the story, couldn't help but answer, "The first." Yet, they failed to realize that Jesus was holding up a mirror to their souls. With piercing insight, Jesus revealed the heart of the matter: the tax collectors and prostitutes, once defiant but now repentant, were entering the Kingdom of God ahead of the self-righteous leaders. These leaders had heard John the Baptist, witnessed the transformations, yet they neither repented nor believed. (Matthew 21:31-32)

Parable of the Vineyard

Building upon the foundation of His previous teaching, Jesus wove another tale, drawing from the imagery familiar to those steeped in agrarian culture. "Hear another parable," He began, "There was a landowner who planted a vineyard, put a fence around it, dug a winepress in it, and built a watchtower. Then he leased it to tenant farmers and went on a journey." Through these words, He spoke of a master's trust and expectation from his stewards, setting the stage for what was to unfold. (Matthew 21:33)

As the tale progressed, it highlighted the repeated refusal of the husbandmen to honor their agreement. When the householder sent servants to collect the fruits, they were beaten, killed, and stoned. Determined to reach an agreement, the householder eventually sent his son, thinking, "They will reverence my son." Yet, this tragic tale reached its climax as the son was cast out of the vineyard and slain. (Matthew 21:34-39)

Turning to the listeners, Jesus asked, "So when the owner of the vineyard comes, what will he do to those tenant farmers?" Their reply, perhaps spoken with a hint of self-righteous indignation or perhaps with genuine shock, echoed the judgment they unknowingly pronounced on themselves: "He will miserably destroy those wicked men." Jesus then astutely quoted scripture, referencing the cornerstone the builders rejected, a prophecy from Psalm 118:22-23. With this, He subtly yet unmistakably identified Himself as the very cornerstone. "So I tell you, the Kingdom of God will be taken away from you and given to a people who will produce its fruit." The gravity of the situation was palpable. (Matthew 21:40-43)

The chief priests and Pharisees, perceiving that Jesus spoke of them, were consumed with indignation and plotted against Him. But they also feared the masses, for the people saw Jesus as a prophet. The link between the parable and Israel's history, where God sent prophets to correct and guide them, and their constant rejection of these prophets, was unmistakable. Their ancestors had mistreated the prophets, and now they were on the brink of doing the same to the Messiah, the Son of God. (Matthew 21:45-46)

Chapter 22

Royal Invitations

Between Faith and Fear: A City on Edge

Jerusalem was a city of contrasts, a tapestry of emotions interwoven by faith, hope, and a heavy air of anticipation. The events of the preceding days had set the city abuzz. Whispers filled the marketplaces, homes, and even the sacred corridors of the temple. The chief priests and elders wore masks of calm authority, but beneath lay simmering resentment and plotting. The populace, however, looked on with wide-eyed wonder. Was this Jesus of Nazareth, the carpenter's son, truly the prophesied Messiah? Their hearts swelled with hope, but also with a cautious anxiety, for they were well aware of the volatile relationship between the religious leaders and this compelling prophet.

The Parable of the Wedding Feast

The King's Invitation and the City's Rejection

Amidst a crowd, Jesus began to narrate a story set in a grand palace, its halls echoing with festive preparations. A king planned a magnificent wedding feast for his son, the heir to his throne. As was the custom, invitations had been sent out well in advance, promising an event of unparalleled splendor. But when the day drew near and the king sent his servants to remind the invited guests, they were met with indifference, even hostility. Some returned with tales of the invitees being too occupied with their farms or businesses, while others bore the scars of violence, having been ill-treated by those they approached. The very city that should've been bustling with anticipation now stood as a symbol of rejection. This was not just a refusal of a royal banquet, but a dismissal of the king's heartfelt offer. (Matthew 22:2-6)

Undeterred by the city's cold response, the compassionate king decided on a different approach. He told his servants, "The feast is prepared, and everything is ready. Go then to the crossroads, the bustling marketplaces, the tranquil countryside, and invite everyone you find, regardless of status or stature." The king's love was so vast that he wanted his banquet halls filled, even if it meant extending the invitation to strangers. The servants, driven by the king's passion, went out, spreading the word far and wide, inviting all, from the rich merchant to the humble farmer, ensuring that the feast would be a true representation of the kingdom's diversity. (Matthew 22:8-10)

The Mixed Gathering and the Man Without a Wedding Garment

As the palace doors opened, a sea of faces poured in, their attire ranging from the richly embroidered to the modestly simple. The air was thick with chatter, laughter, and the delightful aroma of the feast. But amidst the revelry, the king noticed a man without a wedding garment. This was not just about the attire but about the readiness and respect for the occasion. The garment was a symbol of preparation, of having heeded the call in both letter and spirit. Approaching the man, the king questioned his lack of the customary garment. Met with silence, the king, with a heavy heart, ordered him to be cast out, emphasizing that while many are called, few are chosen. This was not a mere tale of a feast; it was a reflection on the state of readiness, of understanding the significance of the call. (Matthew 22:11-14)

Paying Taxes to Caesar
The Pharisees' Plot and Their Disciples' Approach

The Pharisees, well-known for their strict adherence to the Law and their disdain for Roman rule, huddled in whispered discussion. Their irritation with Jesus was evident, for He continually challenged their authority and teachings. A plan began to take shape — they would attempt to entrap Jesus with a politically charged question about taxes. If He supported paying taxes, He would alienate the masses who despised Roman oppression. If He opposed it, He could be reported to the Romans for sedition. With their scheme in place, they sent their disciples, accompanied by the Herodians, to pose as sincere seekers of truth. Approaching Jesus, they began with flattery, "Teacher, we know you are true and teach God's way truthfully. What do you think? Is it lawful to pay taxes to Caesar or not?" (Matthew 22:15-17)

Jesus' Discernment and Response

Jesus, perceiving their malice, saw right through their feigned sincerity. His eyes, filled with a mix of sadness and sternness, met theirs. "Why do you test me, you hypocrites?" He asked, reaching out for a denarius. Holding the coin up, He inquired, "Whose image and inscription is this?" They replied, "Caesar's." In a profound and unexpected response, Jesus said, "Render therefore to Caesar the things that are Caesar's, and to God the things that are God's." His answer was a masterstroke, emphasizing the distinction between earthly and divine responsibilities, and underscoring the deeper allegiance one owes to the Almighty, beyond mere coins and currency. (Matthew 22:18-21)

The Marvel of the Crowd

A hushed silence fell over the crowd. The very air seemed to pause, processing the depth and wisdom of Jesus' words. The Pharisees' disciples and the Herodians were left dumbfounded, their trap rendered useless. The multitude, who had anxiously awaited Jesus' response, now erupted in whispered discussions, their admiration for Him growing. They were in awe of His ability to navigate the complexities of religious and political tension with such clarity and wisdom. Here was a teacher who could not be outwitted, a prophet who spoke with the authority of the Eternal One. (Matthew 22:22)

Question about the Resurrection
The Challenge from the Sadducees

The day was not yet over, and another group approached Jesus, bringing with them another challenge. These were the Sadducees, a sect of Judaism that didn't believe in the resurrection of the dead. Their beliefs starkly contrasted with the Pharisees, and while they held considerable influence in Jerusalem, they were often at odds with other Jewish groups. They came forward with a hypothetical scenario, a story of a woman who had been married to seven brothers, each of whom died without leaving an heir. "In the resurrection, therefore," they asked, trying to corner Jesus, "whose wife will she be of the seven? For they all had her." Their intent was clear: to mock the idea of the resurrection by presenting a seemingly unsolvable dilemma. (Matthew 22:23-28)

Jesus' Insight into the Nature of the Resurrection

Jesus, undeterred and with a serenity that always accompanied His responses, began to address their misconception. "You err," He started, "not knowing the Scriptures nor the power of God." He then unveiled a profound truth about the nature of the resurrection, something that perhaps had never been so clearly articulated before: "For in the resurrection, they neither marry nor are given in marriage, but are like angels in heaven." By this, He was teaching that the nature of existence in the resurrected life is different from the temporal and earthly realities they knew. Marriage, as they understood it, wouldn't exist in the same way. (Matthew 22:29-30)

Confirming the Truth with Scripture

But Jesus didn't stop there. Understanding that the Sadducees held the Torah in high esteem, He referred to the book of Exodus, a text they would not dispute. "Concerning the resurrection of the dead," He continued, "have you not read what was spoken to you by

God, saying, 'I am the God of Abraham, the God of Isaac, and the God of Jacob'?" With this reference, Jesus highlighted that God spoke of the patriarchs as still being, indicating that death wasn't the end. "God is not the God of the dead, but of the living," He concluded. With these words, He not only affirmed the concept of the resurrection but also demonstrated the eternal nature of God's relationship with His people. (Matthew 22:31-32)

The Greatest Commandment
The Pharisee Lawyer's Test

After witnessing the previous exchanges, another group, hearing how Jesus had silenced the Sadducees, approached Him. Among them was a lawyer, well-versed in the laws of Moses, a scholar of the highest rank. With a motive to test Jesus, he inquired, "Master, which is the great commandment in the law?" Such a question was the subject of debate among the religious elite. With 613 commandments in the Torah, determining the "greatest" was no small task. It was a question designed not only to challenge but possibly to trap Jesus, depending on how He might answer. (Matthew 22:34-36)

Jesus' Profound Answer and the Essence of the Law

In His response, Jesus reached back to the very heart of the scriptures, distilling the essence of the entire law and all teachings into two profound commandments. He declared, "You shall love the Lord your God with all your heart, and with all your soul, and with all your mind." directly referencing Deuteronomy 6:5. This command, Jesus said, was the "first and great commandment." But He didn't stop there. He continued, "And the second is like it: You shall love your neighbor as yourself." harkening to Leviticus 19:18.

With profound simplicity, Jesus emphasized love — love for God and love for one's fellow humans — as the core essence of the entire scripture.

In His concluding words, He made the sweeping significance of these two commands clear: "All the laws and teachings of the prophets are based on these two commandments." By this, Jesus taught that all the extensive laws, rituals, and teachings of the scriptures fundamentally pointed to these two principles of love. (Matthew 22:37-40)

Whose Son Is the Christ?
Jesus' Question to the Pharisees

As they gathered, still reeling from His answers, Jesus turned the tables by posing a question of His own. Addressing the Pharisees, He asked, "What do you believe about Christ? Whose son is He?" It was a question that delved deep into their knowledge and understanding of the Scriptures. The Pharisees, confident in their scriptural proficiency, promptly responded, "The son of David." It was the accepted belief, drawn from the prophetic writings, that the Messiah would come from the lineage of King David. (Matthew 22:41-42)

Citing David's Psalm and its Implications

But Jesus, always insightful, posed a challenge to their understanding, bringing forth a complexity that hadn't been contemplated before. "How then," Jesus inquired, "does David, under divine inspiration, call him Lord when he says, 'The LORD said to my Lord, 'Sit at my right hand until I make your enemies your footstool?'''" He was citing Psalm 110, a scripture they all knew well. Here, King David referred to the Messiah as "my Lord" — a title typically reserved for someone greater than oneself. This posed a conundrum: If the Messiah was David's descendant, why

did David, in the Psalm, refer to Him with such a title of reverence? (Matthew 22:43-45)

The Unanswerable Mystery and the Leaders' Silence

The Pharisees, so used to debating intricate points of the Law, found themselves stumped. Jesus had presented an aspect of scripture that transcended mere lineage or earthly understanding. It hinted at the divine nature of the Messiah, a mystery they couldn't unravel. The courtyard was filled with a hushed silence, the kind that follows a revelation too profound to immediately grasp. None of the Pharisees could answer Him, and from that moment, a newfound reverence—or perhaps fear—of Jesus' wisdom kept them from daring to confront Him with further questions. (Matthew 22:46)

After That Day

The events of that day cemented Jesus' authority in the eyes of many. With each answer and parable, He had navigated the traps set for Him and had turned them into lessons of faith, love, and the true understanding of the scriptures. His challenges to established thought were not to demean or belittle but to expand understanding and draw His followers closer to the truths of the Kingdom of Heaven. As the sun began to set on that eventful day, there was a palpable change in the air. The Pharisees and the groups that had tried to challenge Him realized that they couldn't outwit Him with words or riddles. From that day on, they ceased questioning Him, and the undercurrents of their plotting grew deeper and more concealed. (Matthew 22:46, expanded context)

CHAPTER 23

WOES AND WARNINGS

Whispers of Truth and Challenge

The sun, though still present, had begun its descent over Jerusalem, casting the city in a warm, golden hue. In quiet pockets of the temple and in hidden corners of the city, people whispered about the teacher from Galilee who had silenced the Pharisees and the Sadducees with His wisdom. The murmurs carried stories of His teachings, of the blind seeing and the lame walking. They spoke of His compassion and of His confrontations. While many were amazed, the religious leaders plotted in the shadows, resentment burning in their hearts.

Yet, Jesus, aware of the brewing storm, remained resolute. He had a message to deliver, one last discourse before the events of the coming days unfolded. As He stood tall, His gaze piercing and His voice firm, He began to address the masses and their leaders.

Jesus on Religious Hypocrisy

In the vast courtyard of the temple, surrounded by massive limestone walls and ornate structures, a crowd had gathered. Mothers holding their children, men of all trades, and curious onlookers, all fixated on Jesus as He began to speak. The air was thick with anticipation. The weight of Jesus' previous encounters with the religious leaders lent a gravity to the moment.

"The scribes and Pharisees," He began, his voice echoing off the walls, "sit in Moses' seat. They possess the authority to teach God's laws handed down through generations. So, practice and observe whatever they tell you." The crowd nodded, understanding the revered position these religious leaders held. "But," Jesus added with emphasis, "do not do what they do. For they preach, but do not practice." Murmurs spread throughout the audience. They were all too familiar with the burdensome regulations and the glaring inconsistencies between the words and actions of some Pharisees. These leaders, dressed in flowing robes with enlarged phylacteries, loved the admiration of the masses but often missed the essence of the laws they championed. (Matthew 23:2-3)

Jesus continued, detailing the Pharisees' penchant for making a show of their religiosity. "They tie up heavy burdens, hard to bear, and lay them on the shoulders of others; but they themselves are unwilling to lift a finger to move them." The image was clear; these leaders were adding to the weight of the people's spiritual loads without offering genuine guidance or relief. Their actions were rooted not in a true desire to draw people closer to God, but in a deep-seated need for recognition. "They love the place of honor at banquets, greetings in the marketplaces, and to be called 'Rabbi' by others." Yet, in God's Kingdom, such honor-seeking would not be the way. Jesus instructed the crowd, "But you are not to be called 'Rabbi,' for you have one teacher, and you are all students. And call no one your father on earth, for you have one Father—the one in heaven. Nor are you to be called instructors, for you have one instructor, the Messiah." It was a call to humility, a reminder that true greatness in the eyes of the Eternal One was not achieved by exalting oneself, but by serving others. "The greatest among you will be your servant. All who exalt themselves will be humbled, and all who humble themselves will be exalted." (Matthew 23:4-12)

The Seven Woes
Woe to Barriers of the Kingdom

As Jesus' words resonated throughout the courtyard, there was an undeniable tension in the air. The Pharisees and scribes, traditionally respected and unchallenged, now stood in the searing spotlight of Christ's rebuke. He looked at them intently, His gaze unwavering. "Woe to you, scribes and Pharisees, hypocrites!" Jesus exclaimed. "For you shut the door of the Kingdom of Heaven in people's faces. You yourselves do not enter, nor will you let those enter who are trying to." The crowd was stunned. These leaders,

who should be guiding the lost towards God, were likened to gatekeepers turning away seekers. The realization was harrowing: they were barriers to the very Kingdom they preached about. (Matthew 23:13)

Woe to the Misguided Oath-Takers

Shifting His focus to another practice, Jesus addressed their convoluted system of oath-taking. "Woe to you, blind guides!" He said with a tinge of sorrow, "You say, 'If anyone swears by the temple, it means nothing; but anyone who swears by the gold of the temple is bound by that oath.'" The crowd murmured; they had witnessed such twisted logic, where religious leaders placed more importance on the gold adorning the temple than the temple itself, which represented God's presence. By misdirecting reverence, they undermined the sacredness of their own religious institution. (Matthew 23:16-17)

Woe to the Neglecters of Justice, Mercy, and Faith

But Jesus didn't stop there. His voice, firm with righteous indignation, pointed out their skewed priorities. "Woe to you, scribes and Pharisees, hypocrites! You give a tenth of your spices—mint, dill, and cumin. But you have neglected the more important matters of the law—justice, mercy, and faithfulness."

It was a damning assessment. While they meticulously followed certain rituals, they overlooked the very essence of God's law, which prioritized compassion and justice over ritualistic precision. (Matthew 23:23)

Woe to the Outwardly Righteous

Drawing a vivid picture, Jesus continued, "You clean the outside of the cup and dish, but inside they are full of greed and self-indulgence." The metaphor was clear; like a vessel appearing clean on the outside but filthy within, these leaders presented an outward image of righteousness while harboring inner corruption. This surface-level piety deceived many, but not Jesus. (Matthew 23:25)

Woe to Those Blind to Inner Transformation

He then tackled their failure to understand true transformation. "Woe to you, scribes and Pharisees, hypocrites! You are like whitewashed tombs, which look beautiful on the outside but on the inside are full of the bones of the dead and everything unclean." Just as tombs conceal death, these religious leaders masked their spiritual decay with a façade of purity. It was a haunting image, challenging them to look beyond external rites and seek genuine heart change. (Matthew 23:27)

Woe to Those Who Honor Prophets Yet Perpetuate Their Ancestors' Crimes

Finally, addressing their hypocrisy, Jesus remarked, "You build tombs for the prophets and decorate the graves of the righteous. And you say, 'If we had lived in the days of our ancestors, we would not have taken part with them in shedding the blood of the prophets.'" Yet, their very actions and intentions towards Jesus, a prophet in their midst, exposed them. They might honor prophets of old, but they perpetuated their ancestors' crimes by opposing the living Word before them. (Matthew 23:29-32)

Lament Over Jerusalem
A Warning of Impending Judgment

As His discourse reached a crescendo, the intensity of Jesus' voice echoed with both authority and pain. "You serpents, you brood of vipers!" He warned, "How can you escape the condemnation of hell?" Those gathered could feel the weight of His words. He was not merely reprimanding them for their actions; He was forewarning them of the consequences that loomed ahead. This impending judgment would not only affect these leaders but would resonate throughout the city, a place that had witnessed God's interventions countless times but had also repeatedly resisted His calls. The gravity of the situation was palpable, for Jesus was declaring that the city's long-standing rebellion against the Eternal One would culminate in a profound reckoning. (Matthew 23:33)

Yet, amid this stern warning, the tenor of Jesus' voice softened, unveiling a depth of raw emotion. His eyes, perhaps glistening with tears, looked out over the city, the epicenter of God's historical interaction with His people. "O Jerusalem, Jerusalem," He lamented, "the one who kills the prophets and stones those who are sent to her!" His repetition of the city's name emphasized His profound connection and concern. This was not just a geographic location; it was the heart of a people He deeply loved. With an analogy that invoked a tender, maternal imagery, Jesus expressed, "How often I wanted to gather your children together, as a hen gathers her chicks under her wings, but you were not willing!" It was a poignant moment. The Savior of the world, with arms outstretched, longed to embrace and protect His people, just as a hen would shield her young. Yet, they resisted, choosing their own path instead of the refuge He offered. The magnitude of His love contrasted sharply with the city's repeated rejections. (Matthew 23:37)

Chapter 24

When Stones Fall

A Whisper of Change: Before the Prophecy Unfolds

The air was thick with tension, a brooding quiet after the confrontations and lamentations of recent days. Jerusalem, the beloved city with its rich history, stood bathed in the golden hues of sunset, seemingly at peace, but beneath its surface, the currents of change were building. The temple's majestic silhouette, a symbol of faith and tradition, cast long shadows across the city. However, it was this very symbol that would prompt a profound conversation about what lay beyond the horizon of time.

The Temple's Fate
The Magnificence of the Temple

The disciples, marveling at the magnificent architecture of the temple, pointed out its intricate details. Its tall columns, ornate carvings, and the shimmer of gold which adorned its walls reflected the immense wealth and dedication of the Jewish nation to their place of worship. The temple was not just a building; it was the heart of Jerusalem, a testament to their devotion and their history with the Eternal One. As they walked its precincts, the disciples, with a sense of pride, wanted Jesus to acknowledge this marvel, a symbol of their faith and heritage. (Matthew 24:1)

The Prophecy of Desolation

However, Jesus, with a depth of vision far beyond the physical, looked upon the temple with a mix of sorrow and foresight. His voice, steady yet filled with an underlying tone of grief, echoed His prophecy. As the disciples awaited words of admiration, they were met with a revelation that shook their very core. The very stones they admired, Jesus foretold, would soon be in disarray, a desolation that would leave the temple, and thereby their religious world, in ruins. The disciples, taken aback, struggled to comprehend the gravity of such a prediction against the backdrop of the temple's grandeur. (Matthew 24:2)

Signs of the End Times
The Disciples' Earnest Inquiry

Seated on the Mount of Olives, a place that offered a panoramic view of the temple complex and the city beyond, the disciples turned to Jesus. Their hearts weighed with His earlier prophecy, they posed a question that mirrored the angst and curiosity of every believer across the ages: "When will this happen, and what will be the sign of Your coming and the end of the age?" They sought clarity, an understanding of the timeline and the events that would prelude the culmination of history. (Matthew 24:3)

The Rise of Deception and False Prophets

Jesus began by warning them of the rampant deception that would mark these times. "Take heed," He said, "that no one deceives you." He foretold of many coming in His name, claiming to be the Christ, and leading many astray. These false prophets, with their cunning words and feigned miracles, would mimic the truth, attempting to tarnish the essence of the Gospel. It was a call for vigilance, for the world would be rife with duplicity. (Matthew 24:4-5)

Wars, Rumors, and Natural Disasters

Beyond the religious realm, the world itself would be in upheaval. Nations would rise against nations, kingdoms against kingdoms. Wars and their looming threats would be the constant undertone of these times. Yet, these, Jesus mentioned, were just the "be-

ginning of sorrows." Alongside man-made disasters, nature too would be in rebellion: famines, pestilences, and earthquakes in various places would serve as somber markers on the timeline to the end. (Matthew 24:6-8)

Persecutions and the Gospel Proclamation

Believers would bear the brunt of this chaotic world. They would be persecuted, hated by all nations for Jesus' name. Many, under the weight of this persecution, would turn away from the faith and betray one another. Sin would be rampant, causing the love of many to grow cold. However, amidst this turmoil, there would be a beacon of hope – the Gospel of the kingdom would be proclaimed throughout the world as a testimony to all nations. Only after this universal proclamation would the end come. This was the promise of the culmination of their faith and the heralding of a new era. (Matthew 24:9-14)

The Abomination of Desolation
The Prophecy Foretold

Jesus, continuing His discourse, broached a prophecy that had puzzled many – the abomination of desolation, spoken of by the prophet Daniel. He urged understanding and discernment, for when this abomination stood in the holy place, it would be a sign like no other. This sacrilege, a direct affront to God within His holy sanctuary, would signal severe times ahead. Those familiar with the scriptures would recognize the gravity of this sign and the tribulation it heralded. (Daniel 9:27; Matthew 24:15)

Urgency to Flee

With the occurrence of this sign, urgency was paramount. Those in Judea were instructed to flee to the mountains without hesitation. Such would be the immediacy of the situation that those on their rooftops shouldn't descend to gather their belongings, and those in the fields shouldn't turn back to fetch their cloaks. It would be a particularly grievous time for pregnant women and nursing mothers, signaling the harshness of the days. This flight would be the

only respite from the unprecedented tribulation to follow. (Matthew 24:16-19)

Prayers for Favorable Conditions

Jesus asked them to pray that their escape wouldn't be during the winter or on the Sabbath. In these specific conditions, their journey would be even more arduous. The intensity of the tribulation would be unmatched in history and would never be equaled again. If those days weren't shortened, no human would survive. But for the sake of the elect, the chosen of God, those days would be limited. (Matthew 24:20-22)

The Rise of False Prophets and Messiahs

In these treacherous times, deception would reach its zenith. False Christs and false prophets would emerge, showcasing great signs and wonders. Their intent? To deceive, if possible, even the very elect of God. Again, Jesus emphasized vigilance and discernment. He left them with a directive: if they were told of the Christ being in the desert or in inner rooms, they shouldn't believe it. For His return would be unmistakable, like lightning that flashes from the east and illuminates even the west. (Matthew 24:23-27)

The Certainty of His Return

Drawing an analogy from nature, Jesus said that just as vultures gather around a carcass, so will the signs be evident at His coming. There won't be room for doubt or debate; His return would be palpable, evident, and undeniable. (Matthew 24:28)

The Coming of the Son of Man
The Celestial Upheaval

After the tribulation's intense ordeal, the very fabric of the universe would shift. The sun, usually radiant in its brilliance, would darken. The moon, the night's gentle luminary, would fail to give its light. Stars, those distant fixtures of the night sky, would plummet from the heavens. The celestial bodies, which had been constants since the dawn of creation, would be shaken from their ordained paths, signaling the magnitude of the events unfolding on Earth. The entire cosmos would bear witness to these cataclysmic changes, heralding the imminent arrival of the Son of Man. (Matthew 24:29)

The Appearance of the Sign

In the midst of this celestial chaos, a sign would manifest in the sky. This sign, though unspecified, would be undeniable and universally visible. It would be a beacon, a cosmic announcement of the impending arrival of the Son of Man. All tribes of the Earth, irrespective of their location or allegiance, would see it. There would be a collective mourning, a realization of the magnitude of what's about to unfold. The world, in all its diversity, would witness this sign and understand its implication. (Matthew 24:30)

The Majestic Arrival

And then, breaking through the disarray, the Son of Man would appear in the sky. He wouldn't arrive quietly or inconspicuously. His arrival would be grand, accompanied by the loud call of a trumpet. Angels, those celestial beings of power and might, would be dispatched to the four corners of the Earth. Their mission? To gather the elect, God's chosen from every nation and tongue, bringing them into the presence of the Son of Man. This divine roundup would transcend barriers, distances, and dimensions, uniting God's chosen in a singular, epochal event. (Matthew 24:31)

Parables and Lessons of Vigilance
The Lesson from the Fig Tree

Drawing from the natural world around them, Jesus shared the parable of the fig tree. Just as one can determine the approach of summer by the tender branches and new leaves of a fig tree, so too could the signs He described indicate the nearness of the end times. This wasn't just a prediction for a distant future; the generation present would witness the unfolding of these events. While heaven and earth might pass away, the words of the Eternal One, spoken through Jesus, would never fade or falter. However, the exact timing of these events, known only to the Father, remained a divine mystery. (Matthew 24:32-36)

Days of Noah and the Sudden Coming

Jesus then transported the minds of His listeners back to an ancient time - the days of Noah. The people of that era went about their daily routines, oblivious to the impending deluge. Despite Noah's warnings, they were unprepared for the flood that came suddenly upon them. Similarly, the return of the Son of Man would be unexpected. Two people might be working together or sleeping side by side; one would be taken, and the other left behind. Therefore, constant vigilance and readiness were imperative, for the Son of Man would come at an hour least expected. (Matthew 24:37-44)

The Importance of Watchfulness

Stressing the importance of being alert, Jesus posed a scenario: If a homeowner knew when a thief planned to break into his home, he would stay awake and thwart the intrusion. In the same vein, the disciples needed to be on guard, always watchful, for they did not know the day their Lord would return. This was not a call to fear but to faithful anticipation and preparedness. (Matthew 24:43-44)

The Faithful Servant
The Faithful and Wise Servant

Drawing a portrait of responsibility, Jesus described a faithful and wise servant, appointed by his master to oversee his household and provide timely meals for its members. Such a servant, consistently doing his master's will even in his absence, would be blessed. Upon the master's unexpected return, he would find the servant dutifully at work, leading to the servant's promotion over all the master's possessions. (Matthew 24:45-47)

The Wicked Servant's Deception

In stark contrast, another servant, labeled wicked, misjudged the master's return, thinking it delayed. This miscalculation led to a descent into debauchery, as he mistreated his fellow servants and indulged in excesses with drunkards. The day of reckoning, however, was inevitable. The master, returning on a day the servant did not anticipate, meted out severe judgment, cutting him off and assigning him a place with the hypocrites, where there would be weeping and gnashing of teeth. (Matthew 24:48-51)

As Jesus' teachings drew to a close, a reflective silence enveloped the disciples. They had been presented with a profound truth about the future, one that demanded readiness, faithfulness, and utmost vigilance. The contrasting narratives of the faithful and wicked servants served as a stark reminder of the choices they would face in their own journeys. For many of them, the thought of the end times was both awe-inspiring and daunting. Questions swirled in their minds: Would they stand firm in the face of trials? Would they remain faithful to the teachings they had received? The atmosphere was thick with introspection as each disciple contemplated the weight of their calling and the immense responsibility of being prepared for the coming of the Son of Man.

CHAPTER 25

PARABLES
OF
PREPARATION

Dawn of Understanding: Preparing for His Coming

The sun was setting over Jerusalem, painting the sky with hues of oranges and purples. The disciples, still absorbing the teachings from earlier, found a quiet corner in the olive grove. Peter, breaking the silence, voiced the uncertainty many felt, "His words are heavy with meaning, speaking of times I find hard to envision." John, always reflective, responded, "Yet every word is a call to readiness. For a future, though shrouded in mystery, is certain to unfold." It was in this atmosphere of contemplation and reflection that Jesus continued His teachings.

As the sun began its descent, casting the surroundings in a golden hue, Jesus, sensing the apprehension in His disciples following the forewarnings of the end times, decided to share a parable. Their faces, filled with a mix of curiosity and concern, turned to Him as He began to weave a story, aiming to paint a vivid picture of vigilance and preparation.

The Parable of the Ten Virgins
The Anticipation

In a time gone by, Jesus began, his voice steady, yet filled with passion, "The Kingdom of Heaven could be likened unto ten virgins. They took their lamps and went out to meet the bridegroom, an honored and much-awaited figure." The listeners could almost see the young women,

dressed in their finest, waiting in the twilight, their lamps glowing softly against the darkening sky. (Matthew 25:1)

A Delayed Bridegroom and Dwindling Oil

"As the night wore on, the bridegroom tarried, and they all, weary from the wait, slumbered and slept. But at the darkest hour, when the night was still and the world seemed to hold its breath, a cry shattered the silence: 'Behold, the bridegroom cometh; go ye out to meet him!'" Jesus' voice echoed, causing a few disciples to shift uneasily, imagining the urgency of that call. Yet, as the virgins rose and prepared their lamps, half of them faced a dire realization. Their oil was depleted. (Matthew 25:5-8)

The Desperate Plea and The Closed Door

"The five foolish virgins, in their desperation, turned to their wise counterparts, begging, 'Give us of your oil; for our lamps have gone out.' But the wise virgins, knowing the limited supply, responded, 'Not so; lest there be not enough for us and you. Go ye rather to them that sell, and buy for yourselves.'" As the five foolish virgins rushed to find oil, the bridegroom arrived, and those who were ready went in with him to the marriage. The door was shut. By the time the others returned, it was too late. They cried out, 'Lord, Lord, open to us!' But he answered, 'Verily I say unto you, I know you not.'" Jesus paused, letting the weight of the missed opportunity and the finality of the closed door sink in. The disciples exchanged glances, sensing the profound meaning behind the story. (Matthew 25:9-12)

The Solemn Warning

"So, watch therefore," Jesus concluded, his gaze intense, piercing into the very souls of his listeners, "Because you don't know the exact day or hour when the Son of Man will come" The silence that followed was palpable. The disciples realized that this was not just a story. It was a call to vigilance, a call to be prepared, always. (Matthew 25:13)

The Parable of the Talents

Still holding the attention of His disciples, Jesus, discerning their thirst for further understanding, continued with another story. The sun had sunk lower now, the warm oranges giving way to cooler purples, and the soft chirping of the evening crickets began to accompany His voice. He took a moment, his gaze distant, as if viewing the scenes He was about to describe, and then began.

"For the Kingdom of Heaven," Jesus began, "is as a man traveling into a far country, who called his own servants and entrusted his wealth to them." The disciples could visualize a grand estate, the master summoning his trusted servants, and handing over bags filled with shimmering gold coins to each according to

their abilities. One received five talents, another two, and another, just one. (Matthew 25:14-15)

"With the master gone, the first two servants got to work. The one with five talents traded and doubled his amount, as did the one with two talents. Yet, the servant with the single talent, driven by fear, dug a hole and buried his master's money." The scene painted a vivid picture of bustling markets, deals being struck, and coins changing hands, contrasted with the solitary figure of the third servant, cautiously hiding his talent in the earth. (Matthew 25:16-18)

"After a long time, the master of those servants returned, and a reckoning was at hand." Jesus' tone was serious, emphasizing the gravity of the moment. "The first two servants proudly presented their earnings, and their master, pleased with their diligence, declared, 'You've done well, my good and faithful servant. You've been faithful with a few things, and now I will entrust you with many things. Enter into the joy of your Lord.'" The disciples could feel the warmth of the master's approval and the pride of the servants. "However, when the third servant explained his actions, attributing them to his fear of the master's harshness and handing back the single talent, the atmosphere turned cold." (Matthew 25:19-25)

Consequences of Inaction

"The master's face darkened," Jesus continued, the gravity in His voice deepening. "Labeling the servant as wicked and slothful, he ordered the single talent to be taken away and given to the one with ten. He proclaimed, 'To those who already have, more will be given, and they will have an abundance. But from those who have nothing, even what they have will be taken away.' Regarding the unproductive servant, he was thrown into the outer darkness, a place where there will be crying and grinding of teeth." The disciples felt the weight of the judgment and the severe consequences of inaction. (Matthew 25:26-30)

The evening air had grown cooler, and the first stars began to twinkle in the dusky sky. The disciples, engrossed in Jesus' teachings, leaned in closer. He took a deep breath, knowing the gravity of the next revelation.

The Sheep and the Goats

The Majestic Throne and the Gathering of Nations

"When the Son of Man comes in His glory, and all the holy angels with Him," Jesus began, his voice resonating with authority, "then He will sit on the throne of His glory." His followers tried to fathom the scene: A grand, celestial throne, the sky illuminated with countless angels, and nations of every tongue and tribe gathered before it. The majesty was awe-inspiring. (Matthew 25:31)

The Great Separation

"Before Him will be gathered all the nations, and He will separate people one from another, as a shepherd separates the sheep from the goats." The disciples could picture the scene - a vast sea of humanity, and the Son of Man, discerning, positioning the righteous (the sheep) to His right hand, the place of honor, and the unrighteous (the goats) to His left. (Matthew 25:32-33)

The Blessed Inheritance

"To those on His right," Jesus continued, his voice softening with affection, "the King will declare, 'Come, you blessed of My Father, inherit the Kingdom prepared for you from the foundation of the world.'" The disciples could sense the profound love and joy in those words. The reason? "For I was hungry and you gave me food, I was thirsty and you gave me drink, I was a stranger and you welcomed me, I was naked and you clothed me, I was sick and you visited me, I was in prison and you came to me." The criteria were clear: simple acts of genuine love and kindness. (Matthew 25:34-36)

The Profound Revelation

"But when did we see you in these states and serve you?" they might ask. To which the King would reply, "Truly I tell you, whatever you did for one of the least of these brothers and sisters of mine, you did for me." It was a profound revelation. Every act of kindness, no matter how small or to whom it was shown, was an act done to the Lord Himself. (Matthew 25:37-40)

The Dire Consequences for the Unrighteous

However, for those on His left, the scene was grave. The King would declare, "Depart from me, you cursed, into the eternal fire prepared for the devil and his angels." Their sin? Neglecting the very acts of kindness He had mentioned. And the consequences were eternal. The disciples felt the weight of these words and the importance of living righteously in a world filled with need. (Matthew 25:41-46)

The implications of the story were profound: The Eternal One was watching, and the day of reckoning would come. Acts of compassion and love, especially to the downtrodden, were not just good deeds; they were service to the I AM Himself. And the disciples, absorbing this truth, recognized the profound responsibility they held.

CHAPTER 26

THE PASSOVER PROMISE

Shadows of What's to Come

As the sun set over Jerusalem, the atmosphere was dense with anticipation. Jesus had just finished His teachings on the end times, and a silent contemplation had taken over His disciples. They clustered around Him, feeling the gravity of His words but yet unaware of the profound significance of the events that were about to unfold. Whispers of prophecy, tales of old, and the mysterious parables of Jesus hung in the air, like pieces of a puzzle yet to be assembled. For the disciples, the future was vast and uncertain, but they clung to every word Jesus spoke, seeking to understand. Little did they know that the shadows lengthening across the city's streets were also stretching across the very fate of their Master. The bridge between prophecy and fulfillment was about to be crossed, and Jerusalem would be its epicenter.

The Plot Against Jesus

The city of Jerusalem was abuzz with preparations for the Passover, one of the grandest festivals of the Jewish calendar. Homes were being cleaned, and families made ready to remember the ancient deliverance of Israel from Egypt's grasp. Amidst this backdrop of celebration and remembrance, darker plans were being hatched in the very heart of the religious establishment.

In a room, dimly lit by the flickering flames of oil lamps, the high priest Caiaphas convened a secret council with the elders. Their robes whispered secrets as they moved, and their voices, though hushed, carried the weight of their malicious intent. "This Jesus," Caiaphas began, a sneer evident in his voice, "has become a thorn in our side. His popularity grows day by day, and if we don't act now, He might sway the entire city and endanger our position."

Nods of agreement circled the room. But they had a problem. With the city swelling with pilgrims for the Passover, capturing Jesus amidst his many supporters would undoubtedly lead to an uproar. "Not during the feast," one elder cautioned, his fingers stroking his beard thoughtfully, "lest there be an uproar among the people." (Matthew 26:5) The room was filled with a tense silence as they contemplated their next move.

Outside, the night was still, save for the occasional distant sounds of Passover preparations. But within those ancient walls, the decision to end an innocent man's life was taking shape. The stage was set for one of the most significant events in human history, and the shadows of betrayal were beginning to lengthen.

The Anointing at Bethany

In the tranquil town of Bethany, not too far from the bustling streets of Jerusalem, nestled a house that became the scene of an intimate and prophetic moment. Simon the leper, once an outcast but now restored, had opened his home in honor of Jesus. The room was filled with the soft glow of oil lamps and the murmur of conversations, as disciples and guests reclined around the table.

As they dined, a woman approached Jesus with a sense of purpose in her eyes. She held an alabaster jar of very costly fragrant oil. The room's chatter began to fade as all eyes turned to her. With a gentle motion, she broke the jar and began to pour the fragrant oil on Jesus' head. The aroma, rich and sweet, wafted through the room, its scent wrapping around every individual, marking the moment in their memories.

The disciples, particularly Judas Iscariot, watched with growing indignation. "Why this waste?" Judas exclaimed, a hint of greed in his eyes. "This could have been sold for a high price and the money given to the poor." (Matthew 26:8-9) His words echoed the sentiments of some others in the room.

Yet Jesus, always discerning the heart's intentions, came to the woman's defense. "Why do you trouble the woman? For she has done a good work for Me. The poor you have with you always, but Me you do not have always. In pouring this fragrant oil on My body, she did it for My burial." (Matthew 26:10-12) There was a weighty pause, as the significance of His words sunk in.

He continued, "Assuredly, I say to you, wherever this gospel is preached in the whole world, what this woman has done will also be told as a memorial to her." (Matthew 26:13) The room was enveloped in a hushed reverence. Beyond the act's immediate beauty, they began to grasp its prophetic significance, foreshadowing the imminent events that would change the course of history.

Judas Agrees to Betray Jesus

The echoes of Jesus's rebuke from the anointing incident at Bethany were still fresh in the minds of those present. To many, the scene was a poignant testament to devotion and prophecy, but to Judas Iscariot, it was a sting, a reminder of Jesus's words defending the woman's actions. The very act that Jesus had commended felt to Judas like a public chastisement, a perceived waste of expensive perfume that could have been sold to benefit the poor. That offense, combined with whatever other motives darkened his heart, propelled him towards a fateful decision.

Not far from Simon's home, Judas, one of the twelve disciples, made his way into the shadowy corridors of the chief priests. "What are you willing to give me if I deliver Him to you?" (Matthew 26:15) he inquired. The priests, eagerly seizing the opportunity, counted out thirty pieces of silver. A transaction was made, and Judas, with the weight of the coins and the gravity of his impending betrayal, sought the opportune moment to hand Jesus over, far from the watchful eyes of the crowds. The divine narrative continued to unfold, as the pieces of a celestial puzzle clicked into place.

The Eve of Covenant and Betrayal

The glow of the setting sun gave way to the soft hues of twilight over Jerusalem. The city was abuzz with preparations for the imminent Passover, a solemn festival that commemorated Israel's liberation from Egyptian bondage. But on this eve of Passover, the 13th day of Nisan, something profound was taking place.

In a house in the heart of the city, a table was being set. The air was filled with the aroma of freshly cooked food, though the traditional Passover lamb was absent, as this was not the Passover meal but a special supper on the night preceding it. The disciples, still reeling from the revelation of betrayal among them and the poignant event at Bethany, gathered with Jesus, perhaps hoping for a moment of fellowship before the festival's formalities commenced.

As they reclined, enjoying their pre-Passover meal, an intense moment arose. Jesus, with a heavy heart, revealed, "Truly, I tell you, one of you will betray me." (Matthew 26:21) The disciples, taken aback, individually voiced their disbelief, "Surely not I, Lord?" (Matthew 26:22) To which Jesus gave an enigmatic hint, "The one who has dipped his hand into the bowl with me will betray me." (Matthew 26:23)

Judas, perhaps trying to deflect any suspicion, echoed the other disciples, "Surely it isn't me, Rabbi?" Jesus met his gaze, and calmly replied, "You have said so." (Matthew 26:25)

But the evening held another profound moment. Jesus took bread, blessed it, broke it, and distributed it among His disciples, saying, "Take, eat; this is my body." (Matthew 26:26) Then, taking a cup filled with wine, He pronounced, "Drink from it, all of you. This is my blood of the covenant, which is poured out for many for the forgiveness of sins." (Matthew 26:27-28) This act was significant, embedding the essence of His forthcoming sacrifice into a meal they would remember forever.

As night fully enveloped the city, they sang a hymn together, their voices echoing in the stillness. The group then ventured to the Mount of Olives, unaware that the forthcoming hours would challenge their faith like never before.

The Weight of Foreknowledge

As the embers of the mealtime conversation faded, the room grew solemn, filled with the weight of a new revelation. The atmosphere, thick with intensity, held onto every word Jesus spoke. With a gaze that bore both sadness and understanding, He turned to His disciples.

"All of you will be made to stumble because of me this night, for it is written: 'I will strike the Shepherd, and the sheep of the flock will be scattered.'" (Matthew 26:31) He was referencing the haunting words from the prophet Zechariah, emphasizing the gravity of what lay ahead.

Peter, his spirit always burning with fervor, immediately responded, "Even if everyone else falls away because of You, I will never fall away." (Matthew 26:33) Jesus looked deep into Peter's eyes, His gaze filled with compassion and sadness. "Truly, I tell you, this very night, before the rooster crows, you will deny Me three times." (Matthew 26:34)

Shaken, Peter protested, "Even if I must die with You, I will never deny You!" (Matthew 26:35) The other disciples, inspired by Peter's conviction, echoed his sentiment. Yet, within the depths of Jesus' eyes, there was an understanding that transcended their momentary pledges of loyalty. The night's shadows had only just begun to unveil their truths.

Gethsemane's Anguish

The night had deepened, with the soft glow of torches in the distance casting shadows among the ancient olive trees of Gethsemane. The garden's air, usually filled with the gentle hum of nocturnal life, seemed unusually quiet, as if nature itself held its breath in anticipation of what was to come.

Jesus led His disciples deeper into the garden, the heaviness in His heart palpable. "Stay here and remain vigilant," He told most of them. Taking Peter,

James, and John a little further, they could see the distress on His face, more intense than they had ever witnessed. "My soul is overwhelmed with sorrow to the point of death," He confided in them, "Stay here and keep watch with Me." (Matthew 26:38)

Separating Himself a short distance from the trio, the weight of the world's sin and impending separation from the Eternal One pressed down on Him. He fell to the ground, the coolness of the earth against His forehead. "O my Father," He agonized, the intensity of His plea echoing in the silent grove, "if it is possible, let this cup pass from Me; nevertheless, not as I will, but as You will." (Matthew 26:39)

Time seemed to stretch indefinitely. An hour passed. Jesus, returning to the disciples, found them asleep, the emotional and physical toll of the evening weighing heavily upon them. He nudged Peter, "Couldn't you men keep watch with Me for one hour?" (Matthew 26:40) His voice carried a mix of disappointment and understanding. He admonished them, "Watch and pray, so that you will not fall into temptation. The spirit is willing, but the flesh is weak." (Matthew 26:41)

Yet, twice more, Jesus withdrew to pour His heart out to the Father, each time grappling with the

tremendous burden He was about to bear, and each time, finding His disciples asleep upon His return.

With a final, resolute breath, the moment of decision had arrived. "Behold, the hour is at hand, and the Son of Man is being betrayed into the hands of sinners," He declared to His disciples. (Matthew 26:45) The torchlights were drawing nearer, the hum of voices grew louder, and the footsteps of those coming to arrest Him resonated through the stillness of the garden. The test of Gethsemane was coming to its pivotal climax.

The Arrest

The leaves rustled and the ground echoed with the marching of feet. The usually serene Garden of Gethsemane was now disrupted by the clamor of an approaching mob. The silhouettes of men armed with clubs and swords became increasingly visible in the dim light. At the helm of this multitude was Judas Iscariot, his face betraying a mix of determination and regret. The disciples' eyes darted anxiously from one face to another, trying to understand the gravity of what was unfolding.

Suddenly, Judas stepped forward, his gaze locked onto Jesus. There was a pause that felt like eternity. Without a word, he leaned in and planted a kiss on Jesus' cheek, sealing his betrayal. It was a chilling act, turning a symbol of affection into one of treachery.

The mob surged forward, grabbing Jesus with rough hands, the intent in their eyes clear. Reacting impulsively, Peter, his face red with rage and fear, unsheathed his sword, striking at a servant of the high priest, severing his ear. Blood spattered onto the ground, an unsettling harbinger of the violence to come.

Yet Jesus, calm amidst the chaos, raised His hand in restraint. "Put your sword in its place," He commanded Peter with a stern voice, "for all who take the sword will perish by the sword." (Matthew 26:52) Reaching out, He touched the servant's ear, healing it

instantly, a final miraculous act before His imminent suffering.

His eyes, filled with sorrow yet unwavering, met those of the mob. "Have you come out, as against a robber, with swords and clubs to take Me? I sat daily with you, teaching in the temple, and you did not seize Me. But all this was done that the Scriptures of the prophets might be fulfilled." (Matthew 26:55-56)

The disciples, overwhelmed by the swiftness of the betrayal and the raw display of force, felt panic rise within them. In their confusion and fear, they fled into the darkness, leaving Jesus alone in the hands of His captors. The prophecy was being fulfilled; the Shepherd was struck, and the sheep were scattered.

Jesus Before the Sanhedrin

The once tranquil night had taken a sinister turn. The Gethsemane garden, where moments ago, Jesus had been in deep, soul-wrenching prayer, now seemed distant. The path taken was illuminated only by the dim glow of torches, casting eerie shadows as the group made its way through the narrow, stone-laden streets of Jerusalem.

Jesus, hands bound, was pushed and shoved, but He walked with a quiet dignity, a stark contrast to the

harshness of His captors. They led Him to a grand house — the residence of Caiaphas, the high priest. The ambiance within was thick with anticipation. Assembled there was a gathering of Jerusalem's elite: scribes, elders, and other members of the Sanhedrin, the Jewish high council. The room echoed with murmurs and whispers as they eagerly awaited the trial of this man who had so disrupted their traditions and teachings.

One by one, witnesses were brought forth. They spoke against Jesus, their words dripping with animosity. But their accounts conflicted, making it apparent that these were false testimonies conjured to serve a predetermined verdict. The room grew tense as it became clear that a solid case against Jesus was elusive.

Caiaphas, growing impatient and sensing the need to take control, rose from his ornate seat. His voice filled the room as he addressed Jesus directly, "I adjure You by the living God that You tell us if You are the Christ, the Son of God." (Matthew 26:63)

All eyes turned to Jesus, waiting for His response. In the ensuing silence, Jesus finally spoke, "You have said it yourself. But I tell you, from now on you will see the Son of Man seated at the right hand of the

Power and coming on the clouds of heaven." (Matthew 26:64)

This proclamation held a profound significance. By referencing the "Son of Man" and "seated at the right hand of the Power," Jesus was alluding to Daniel's vision, where the prophet spoke of the divine figure that would have dominion over all. "The Right Hand of God" was not about a physical position but represented the pinnacle of supreme authority. In essence, Jesus was declaring His divine identity, asserting that He was God Himself. Caiaphas, recognizing the gravity of this assertion, was consumed by outrage. In a theatrical display, he tore his robes, exclaiming, "He has blasphemed! What further need do we have of witnesses? See, now you have heard His blasphemy!" (Matthew 26:65)

The atmosphere turned from anticipation to outright hostility. Those present spat at Jesus, blindfolded Him, and struck Him, mockingly urging Him to prophesy who had hit Him. As dawn approached, the Son of God endured their scorn and abuse, remaining the calm epicenter of a storm of hatred. The events of that fateful night had only just begun.

Peter's Denial

The grandeur of Caiaphas' residence cast its formidable shadow over the courtyard, where a fire flickered, casting dancing flames that broke the darkness of pre-dawn. Here, a mixed company gathered - guards, servants, and curious onlookers. Among them was Peter, who had stealthily followed Jesus after the arrest, hoping to see what would transpire.

The courtyard had a palpable tension. The chilly night air brought people closer to the fire, its warmth a brief respite from the uncertainty and anxiety of what was unfolding inside the house. Peter, huddled near the flames, tried to blend in, his face partially hidden beneath the hood of his cloak. But a keen-eyed servant girl recognized him, squinting slightly before boldly declaring, "This man was with Jesus the Nazarene!" (Matthew 26:69)

Peter's heart raced. His immediate reaction was one of self-preservation. He denied it, saying, "I don't know what you're talking about." (Matthew 26:70) He moved away, trying to distance himself from the accusing eyes, but the girl persisted, pointing him out to others, "This is one of them!" (Matthew 26:71)

Peter, desperate, denied it again, but with more force, swearing to emphasize his point. Yet, as he tried to blend into the background, another group pressed the assertion, "Surely you too are one of them, for your accent betrays you." (Matthew 26:73)

Fear, and the instinct to survive, drove Peter to vehemently deny knowing Jesus, even invoking a curse upon himself to drive home his claim. No sooner had he done this than the haunting, prophetic sound of a rooster's crow rent the early morning air. The weight of Jesus' earlier words - "Before the rooster crows, you will deny Me three times." (Matthew 26:34) - crashed upon him with the force of a tidal wave.

Peter's world crumbled. His eyes, filled with the realization of his betrayal, searched the surroundings, and, for a fleeting moment, met those of Jesus, who was being moved between rooms. The depth of sorrow in that shared glance was immeasurable.

Overwhelmed by shame and heartbreak, Peter fled the courtyard. He sought solace in the shadows of Jerusalem's narrow alleys, but found none. In the midst of the city's labyrinthine streets, he fell to his knees, the weight of his betrayal breaking him. His anguished cries echoed as he wept bitterly, mourning the disconnect between his earlier vows of loyalty and his actions in the crucible of testing.

CHAPTER 27

DAWN'S DESCENT

Preparing the Lamb: A Passover Like No Other

Passover eve blanketed Jerusalem, a city usually bustling with trade and religious debates. The city streets, usually echoing with joyful preparations for the evening's festivities, were rife with tension. Families prepared their lambs for the evening meal, a symbol of God's mercy in sparing the Israelites from death in Egypt. But unbeknownst to many, the religious leaders were orchestrating a much darker preparation. The same hands that would partake in the Passover meal were conspiring to offer a different Lamb, the Lamb of God, as a sacrifice on this Passover. It wasn't just about a revolutionary or a great teacher anymore. It was about a man who dared to echo eternity's claim, a man who had proclaimed Himself as the Son of God, as the Son of Man, as one with the Eternal One. The claims were sacrilege to the religious elites, a direct challenge to the foundation of their faith and authority. And for those who dared to believe, it was the hope of ages coming alive, the meshing of heaven and earth. Jerusalem stood at the precipice of history, on the cusp of a Passover that would forever redefine its meaning.

Morning's Dark Deal

The morning light tried to pierce through the grey clouds that hung over Jerusalem, yet the city's atmosphere was electric. A day before the Passover, preparations were in full swing. While families readied their homes and looked to the rituals that commemorated their deliverance from Egypt, an entirely diffcrent preparation was underway within the hallowed walls of the Sanhedrin chambers. Instead of preparing a lamb for the Passover meal, these religious leaders were plotting to offer up the Lamb of God as a sacrifice.

Inside, the council's deliberations resonated with echoes of disdain and determination. Jesus, the charismatic preacher from Nazareth, had not only claimed to be the Son of God but had also performed miracles, displayed unparalleled authority over scriptures, and won the hearts of many. He was an affront to their power, a disruptor of their status quo, and they saw Him as a threat to their religious hierarchy. "He made Himself equal to the Eternal One," they whispered among themselves, their tone thick with contempt. Their verdict was clear: Jesus had to be eliminated. With grim faces, they resolved to hand Him over to the Roman governor, Pilate. The religious charge had been set, but they needed a political one to ensure Rome's cooperation. (Matthew 27:1-2)

But not all were at peace with this resolution. Outside the chambers, remorse was etching deep lines on Judas Iscariot's face. He had envisioned many outcomes when he struck the deal with the chief priests, but the real gravity of his betrayal now weighed on him with suffocating force. The thirty silver coins – once a symbol of a profitable transaction – now felt like chains binding his soul. With desperate eyes, he sought out the chief priests and elders, his voice choked with guilt, "I have sinned by betraying innocent blood!" But their cold, calculated eyes met his, their reply a chilling testament to their hard hearts, "What is that to us? See to it yourself." (Matthew 27:3-4)

This final rejection, the clear dismissal of his anguish, was the last straw for Judas. The streets of Jerusalem, bustling with Passover preparations, became a blur as he threw the blood money into the temple and sought refuge from the relentless torment of his conscience, ending his life in utter despair. (Matthew 27:5)

Meanwhile, the chief priests, always meticulous in matters of the law, looked upon the scattered silver with disdain. Deeming it inappropriate for temple coffers due to its association with blood money, they collectively decided to purchase the potter's field as a burial place for strangers. In doing so, they unknowingly fulfilled a prophecy by Jeremiah, a testament to the Divine's overarching narrative, even amidst humanity's darkest moments. "And they took the thirty pieces of silver... and gave them for the potter's field, as the Lord directed me." (Matthew 27:6-10)

Pontius Pilate: Between Power & Principle

The grandeur of the praetorium stood in stark contrast to the tension that hung in the air. Roman banners, displaying the might of the empire, fluttered outside, while inside, the cool, shadowed hall echoed with a quiet intensity. At the heart of it all was Pontius Pilate, the Roman governor. Stern, pragmatic, and accustomed to the power his position held, he now found himself at a crossroads.

A hush fell as Jesus, hands bound, was brought forward. Pilate's discerning eyes assessed the figure before him. This was the man causing so much commotion? He seemed so... ordinary. Without preamble, he posed the question burning in his mind, "Are You the King of the Jews?" The air seemed to thicken as Jesus responded with calm assurance, "It is as you say." (Matthew 27:11)

However, outside this chamber of judgment, a different scene played out. The chief priests and elders, with their insidious influence, were at work. They whispered into the ears of the gathered masses, spinning a narrative that painted Jesus as a threat to their traditions and to Rome itself. The crowd, fickle as always and now manipulated, began to roar with demands.

Taking advantage of a customary gesture where a prisoner was released at the Passover festival, Pilate saw an opportunity. He presented them with a choice: Jesus, the proclaimed Son of God, or Barabbas, a known criminal and insurgent. In a stunning turn, the

voices united in clamoring for Barabbas's freedom and Jesus's crucifixion. The very streets that had once echoed with "Hosanna!" now resounded with cries of "Crucify Him!" (Matthew 27:15-23)

Pilate, sensing the volatility of the moment and the mounting pressure from the crowd, sought a way out. But before he took the next step, he made a public declaration. In a symbolic gesture, he brought out a basin of water, washing his hands before the assembled masses. "I am innocent of this man's blood," he proclaimed, distancing himself from the impending act. "It is your responsibility!" (Matthew 27:24)

The crowd, undeterred and now further incensed, replied, "His blood be on us and on our children!" (Matthew 27:25)

With that chilling declaration, Pilate made his decision. Jesus was handed over to the Roman soldiers, and the path to Golgotha was set. Though Pilate might have washed his hands, the tides of history would forever record his role in the events of that fateful Passover eve. (Matthew 27:26)

The Mocking of Majesty

Amidst the cold stone walls of the fortress, the Roman soldiers, resplendent in their armor, gathered in the common hall. Their laughter echoed ominously, contrasting with the somber atmosphere that had taken hold of Jerusalem. These men, representatives of the vast Roman Empire, were unaccustomed to the drama and fervor of the Jewish Passover. To them, the man called Jesus was merely another insurgent, another fleeting story.

As Jesus was thrust into their midst, a wicked idea took root among the soldiers. With rough hands, they stripped Him of His clothes, leaving His battered body exposed to their jeers. From the storeroom, they produced a worn-out scarlet robe – a castoff from some Roman official – and with mocking ceremony, draped it over Jesus' shoulders. The robe, meant to symbolize royalty, hung loose on His bruised form.

Yet their cruelty did not end there. One of the soldiers, possibly recalling the accusations against Jesus – that He claimed to be King – fetched some long, spiky thorns. Twisting them into a makeshift crown, they pressed it down onto Jesus' brow. Drops of blood trickled down, the thorns piercing into His skin, adding to the many wounds that marred His visage.

With mock reverence, they then bowed before Him. "Hail, King of the Jews!" they jeered, their laughter filling the room. Each taunt, each jeer, seemed to amuse them more. They spat upon Him and, taking a reed, struck Him on the head, driving the thorns deeper. This was their sport, their entertainment, seemingly oblivious to the cosmic drama unfolding.

But their malevolent mirth would not last forever. Once they had their fill of this macabre game, they removed the scarlet robe, redressing Him in His own garments. The weight of what was to come hung heavily in the air. Jesus, bearing the marks of their scorn, was then led out, continuing His heart-wrenching journey towards Calvary.

The Cross: Humanity's Darkest & Brightest Moment

An Unexpected Bearer from Cyrene

As Jesus, beaten and bruised, struggled under the weight of the cross, a man named Simon from Cyrene found himself suddenly thrust into the narrative of redemption. Perhaps he had come to Jerusalem as a pilgrim for the Passover, perhaps out of mere curiosity. But that day, the Roman soldiers pulled him from the crowd, forcing him to shoulder the weight of the cross alongside Jesus. Together, the Messiah and this unsuspecting Cyrenian made their way to Golgotha, the Place of the Skull. The weight of the wood was heavy, but the weight of the moment, the realization of its significance, was infinitely heavier.

The Bitter Mockery of the Innocent

The journey to Golgotha was arduous, not just in physical exertion but in the torment of the soul. As they reached the hill, the soldiers, ever so cruel in their amusement, offered Jesus wine mixed with gall — a bitter substance. It was a gesture of mock pity, an insult disguised as mercy. He tasted it, recognizing its bitterness, and refused it. This was not the bitterness of the drink, but the bitterness of humanity's cruelty.

With ruthless efficiency, the soldiers went about their gruesome task. They laid Him down on that rugged cross, each hammer blow echoing the world's rejection of its Savior. As they lifted the cross and secured it into the ground, the agonizing weight of His body tore at the fresh wounds on His hands and feet. And yet, with a love incomprehensible, He looked down upon those who tormented Him and silently offered forgiveness with every labored breath. The crowd watched, some with glee, some with indifference, and others with tear-filled eyes, understanding the enormity of the sacrifice being made before them.

A Title in Irony, A Truth in Eternity

Above Him, on a placard crudely fastened to the wood, read the inscription: "THIS IS JESUS THE KING OF THE JEWS." It was intended as the final jab, a sarcastic tribute to the man they believed was nothing more than a deluded prophet. The scoffing world had given Him this title in mockery, not understanding the profound truth it held.

But in this heart-wrenching tableau, where pain and love intertwined, that very title held a deeper resonance. They had unknowingly declared His rightful position. Jesus, hanging battered and bruised, was indeed the King – not just of the Jews, but of all creation. A King who, in His unparalleled grace, chose the path of ultimate sacrifice for His subjects.

The wind carried the jeers and taunts, but also whispered an eternal truth to those with ears to hear. Amongst the clamor of disdain, this title stood as a beacon of hope for all generations to come. The

world had labeled Him in irony, but heaven and those who understood proclaimed it in reverence. The King had come, not to conquer by might but by love, not to start a rebellion but to offer redemption.

The Thieves: Contrasting Fates Beside the Savior

Flanking Jesus on either side were two thieves, symbols of the sin and transgression He was put between, representative of the very humanity He came to save. Their crosses bore the weight of their misdeeds, yet their proximity to the Savior in this critical moment painted a vivid contrast of destiny.

One thief, hardened and embittered by his life's choices, lashed out at Jesus, joining in the chorus of ridicule. His voice, strained from pain and anger, spat venomous doubts, challenging the Savior to save Himself and them if He truly was the Messiah. He was a reflection of a world that saw but did not perceive, that heard but did not understand.

Yet, the other thief, in his final moments, underwent a transformative epiphany. Recognizing the innocence in Jesus and the divinity of His mission, he rebuked his fellow criminal. With the weight of his sins pressing on his heart and the light of realization dawning in his eyes, he made a poignant plea, "Lord, remember me when You come into Your Kingdom." (Luke 23:42) Here was a man, at the brink of death, seeking a sliver of hope, a touch of mercy.

And in that gravest of hours, even as His own life ebbed away, Jesus, in His infinite compassion, responded, "Truly I tell you, today you will be with Me in paradise." (Luke 23:43) The promise was profound. One thief would descend into oblivion, his voice lost in the winds of time, while the other, despite a life of crime, would ascend to paradise, his plea for mercy echoing through eternity.

These thieves, in their stark divergence of fate, illustrated the overarching narrative of humanity: On one side, skepticism, doubt, and disdain, and on the other, faith, hope, and redemption. At the crossroads of history, beside the Redeemer, they showcased the eternal choice laid before mankind.

Echoes of Mockery: The World's Cold Indifference

As Jesus hung, bloodied and bruised, an agonizing spectacle began beneath His pierced feet. The very streets that had once echoed with shouts of "Hosanna!" now resounded with taunts and jeers. Every sarcastic comment, every disdainful laugh, was a raw wound upon the heart of a Savior who had given all for the very souls that mocked Him.

Passersby shook their heads, their faces contorted with scorn. They threw His own words back at Him, a twisted jest, "You who would destroy the temple and rebuild it in three days, save Yourself!" The irony was thick; little did they realize that the true temple, the very essence of God among men, hung before them, willingly sacrificing Himself for their redemption.

A short distance away, the religious leaders stood, their robes pristine in the afternoon sun. Yet, their hearts were cloaked in darkness. They had witnessed His miracles, heard His teachings, and even felt the stirrings of conviction. But now, pride and envy had turned them into mockers. "He saved others," they sneered, "but He cannot save Himself!" They challenged Him to come down from the cross, promising belief, but in the depths of their hearts, they feared the very possibility.

The weight of these words was not lost on the Savior. He could have, in a breath, proven them all wrong. Yet, He chose love over vindication, salvation over escape. The jeers continued, even from one of the thieves beside Him. The very air seemed heavy with scorn.

But in that torrent of mockery, the true tragedy lay not in the words spoken, but in the redemption being missed. The King of the universe, the embodiment of love and grace, was offering the world its greatest gift. And, in blind ignorance, the world laughed and turned away.

This was not just the ridicule of a man; it was the rejection of hope, the scoffing of love, the denial of grace. The tragedy of the cross was not just in the nails, thorns, or spear; it was in the hardened hearts that witnessed God's love and chose disdain instead.

From Desolation to Triumph
The Darkened Sky

In the vast expanse of Jerusalem's horizon, the sun, that ever-burning beacon of time and light, began to waver. Its radiant glow, which once painted the city with hues of gold, now receded. As though held back by an unseen hand, it dimmed, casting long, somber shadows across the land. The city, abuzz with preparations for the Passover, found itself enveloped in a sudden, chilling shroud of darkness.

Whispers of confusion turned into vocal concerns as midday turned inexplicably into an enigmatic twilight. Streets that should have shimmered under the noonday sun were now cloaked in shades of gray. Lamps were hastily lit, their flickering flames casting an unstable glow, mimicking the uncertainty that gripped every heart.

From the bustling marketplaces to the sacred temple grounds, activities ceased. Children clung to their parents, eyes wide with apprehension. Elders exchanged uneasy glances, recalling the prophecies of old. Was this a sign from the heavens? A divine proclamation, perhaps?

High above, the cosmic orchestra, which had played its continuous melody since the dawn of creation, seemed to hold its breath. Stars, usually hidden by the sun's overpowering brilliance, hesitated in their tracks, as if waiting for a cue. The very air grew thick, charged with anticipation.

And at the epicenter of it all, on a hill not far from the city walls, stood three crosses. On the central one, a figure hung, head bowed. The weight of this moment, the profound grief of the universe, converged upon Him. Heaven and Earth, in a rare, unified lament, mourned for the Son they were losing and the salvation the world was gaining.

The Timing of Destiny

In the heart of Jerusalem, smoke ascended from countless homes, carrying with it the aroma of lambs being prepared. The city's narrow alleys and broad squares echoed with the voices of families rejoicing, children laughing, and the ancient melodies sung in remembrance of a divine intervention from ages past. This was Passover, the sacred festival, a time when every household remembered how the blood of a lamb on their doorposts had once spared their ancestors from death.

But outside the city walls, on a hill known as Golgotha, another scene was unfolding — one of stark contrast and profound significance. The silhouettes of three crosses stood against the dimming sky, and on the central cross hung a man, Jesus of Nazareth. With each painful gasp for breath, He bore the weight not just of the wooden beams, but of humanity's sins and hopes.

Onlookers, some with tears streaming down their faces and others with sneers of disdain, watched as the soldiers nailed Him to the cross. Each hammer's blow seemed to resonate with a deeper meaning, piercing the very fabric of time and space. The ringing metal against metal was not just the sound of a nail piercing wood; it echoed through the corridors of history, fulfilling ancient prophecies and divine promises.

The irony was profound and heartbreaking. As the shadows grew longer and the first stars of evening began to appear, marking the beginning of the 14th of Nisan, the true Passover Lamb was being sacrificed. Just as families began their ritualistic feasts, commemorating their deliverance from bondage, here was the embodiment of divine love, offering Himself for the ultimate deliverance of humanity.

Elders who knew the scriptures might have recalled the words of the prophet Isaiah, "He was oppressed, and He was afflicted, yet He opened not His mouth: He is brought as a lamb to the slaughter..." The threads of destiny, woven through centuries of prophecies and events, now converged at this singular, heart-wrenching moment. As the Lamb of God was being sacrificed, Heaven watched, Earth trembled, and the eternal plan of redemption was being fulfilled.

The Weight of Sin

The ambiance at Golgotha was thick with a tension that went beyond the tangible. Onlookers could see the blood, the sweat, and the anguish etched on Jesus's face, but what they couldn't perceive was the invisible burden that pressed heavily upon His soul. Every lie ever whispered, every act of betrayal, every malicious thought, and every dark deed committed by humanity bore down on Him with an intensity incomprehensible to the finite mind.

As the seconds ticked by, a transformation began. Jesus, the sinless one, started to feel the shadows of wickedness envelop Him. It was as if a dark, suffocating shroud began wrapping around Him, every thread woven from the transgressions of every man, woman, and child. From Adam's first act of disobedience to the final sin that will ever be committed, all were laid upon Him. His radiant soul, which had always resonated in harmony with the pure heart of the Eternal One, now experienced an alien and excruciating dissonance.

The crowd, engulfed in their limited understanding, were oblivious to the cosmic transaction occurring before them. All they saw was a man, beaten and crucified. They couldn't fathom that at that very moment, the most profound act of love was unfolding — an act that would alter the course of eternity.

Suddenly, from His parched lips, emerged a cry so raw and filled with anguish that it pierced the very heavens: "Elohai, Elohai, lama sabachthani?" His voice trembled with the pain of abandonment, a desolation so profound that it echoed through the annals of time. Those nearby, not grasping the depth of His words, thought He was calling out to the prophet Elijah. But in reality, it was a cry that unveiled the heart's torment when the purest soul ever to walk the Earth felt, for the first time, the chill of separation from divine love.

Tears, not just of physical pain but of deep, soul-wrenching sorrow, streamed down His face. The Savior, who had come to reunite humanity with their Creator, was momentarily forsaken so that none would ever have to be. The magnitude of His sacrifice, the vastness of His love, was showcased in that singular, agonizing cry.

The Ultimate Sacrifice

The world seemed to stand still at that moment. There was a heaviness in the air, an acute awareness of the gravity of what was transpiring. Those present, even if they didn't fully understand, could feel that

something monumental was unfolding before their eyes.

The sky, still draped in an unyielding darkness, became the backdrop to the final act of this divine drama. Amidst the bleakness, Jesus hung, His battered body a stark contrast to the serenity that began to wash over His face. Every ounce of pain, every drop of blood shed, every scornful remark hurled at Him — all of it culminated in this pivotal instant.

Silence wrapped Golgotha like a shroud, broken only by the ragged breaths of the Man on the Cross. Then, with a strength that defied His physical state, Jesus lifted His head heavenward. In His eyes, there was no defeat, no resignation. Instead, they sparkled with a mix of determination and profound love.

"It is finished," He declared, His voice resonant with authority and finality. These were not the words of a man defeated, but the proclamation of a King who had accomplished the most significant task ever entrusted to anyone. The weight of the sins of the world, the very purpose of His coming to Earth, had been addressed. Salvation's door had been flung open wide.

And then, with a grace only He could muster, Jesus released His breath into the hands of the Father.

He chose the exact moment, aligning it perfectly with the beginning of Passover. As households across Jerusalem ushered in the festival with the sacrifice of lambs, the true Lamb, the ultimate sacrifice, offered Himself up for all of humanity.

A hush fell, not just on Golgotha, but seemingly on all of creation. The universe had just witnessed the greatest act of love, a love so profound that it willingly embraced death to give life to others. The Savior's mission, a mission of redemption, had been accomplished.

Earthly and Heavenly Reactions

As the last echoes of Jesus' declaration faded, a series of profound, almost otherworldly events began to unfold, transforming the landscape of Jerusalem and shaking the very core of its inhabitants' beliefs.

First came the veil. This wasn't just any fabric but a thick, intricately woven curtain, serving as a barrier in the temple, separating the Holy of Holies – the most sacred space where God's presence dwelled – from the rest of the world. This veil, believed to be impenetrable except by the high priest once a year, began to tear. Not from the bottom, as if tampered with by human hands, but from the top, descending downwards. The tear's very direction hinted at a divine intervention, a powerful statement from the heavens. It was as though the Almighty was proclaiming, "See, the way is now clear! The separation is no more." The chasm between God and man, once vast and insurmountable, had been bridged by the sacrifice of the Lamb.

Then, the earth itself couldn't remain silent. It heaved and groaned, quaking under the magnitude of what had just transpired. The ground shook, its tremors a visceral manifestation of the cosmic significance of Jesus' sacrifice.

But the marvels didn't stop there. Tombs, those silent sentinels of death, began to crack open. It was a promise, a hint of the resurrection power that was to come. These tombs, once holding the remains of the departed saints, would soon see life again. But they would wait, for their resurrection was to follow that of the Firstborn from the dead. They were to be the First Fruits, a testament to Jesus' victory over death and a foretaste of the eternal life He was offering humanity. These saints, once risen, would stand as witnesses to the resurrection power of Christ, testifying to the world of the hope and future He had secured.

Amidst these heavenly signs and wonders, there was a palpable shift in the atmosphere. The dread and sorrow that had blanketed Golgotha began to give way to something else: a dawning realization, a burgeoning hope, and for some, perhaps, the first inklings of belief in the Messiah's transformative power.

A Startling Realization

The aftermath of such a cosmic display was a silence so profound, it was almost tangible. The mournful wails, the jeers, and the noise of the crowd had ceased, replaced by a stunned quiet that blanketed Golgotha. It was as if the very air was holding its breath, waiting for someone to give voice to the magnitude of what had just unfolded.

Amidst this stillness, the rugged figure of a Roman centurion, a man trained for war and hardened by countless battles, stood near the cross, absorbing every detail. His eyes, which had seen many deaths, looked upon the lifeless body of Jesus with a different kind of realization. This wasn't just another man; this was something... more.

The signs in the heavens, the tear in the veil, the quaking earth — all of these had converged into a moment of clarity for this battle-hardened soldier. With a voice, softer and more vulnerable than his comrades had ever heard, he uttered a truth that echoed the sentiments of many who stood there that day: "Truly this was the Son of God."

His declaration was powerful in its simplicity and profound in its understanding. Here was a man of Rome, without prior allegiance to the God of Israel, recognizing the deity of Jesus. It was an acknowledgment that transcended culture, position, and upbringing.

Tears might have streaked the dust on his face as the weight of this realization settled in his heart. Around him, those words may have resonated with others, stirring souls and evoking emotions ranging from regret to newfound faith.

The cross, once a symbol of shame and horror, was now bathed in a new light, a beacon signaling the redemption of humanity. And as the sun began its de-

scent, casting long shadows across Jerusalem, it heralded not an end but a new beginning. The story was far from over. The best was yet to come.

The Compassionate Women & An Honorable Act

The scene at Golgotha was a gut-wrenching tableau of cruelty and pain, yet it was punctuated by the silent strength of devoted hearts. From a distance, shadows of several figures could be seen, women who had followed Jesus from the beginning. Their presence was like a beacon of compassion amid the grotesque panorama of death. The sun, already subdued from the earlier darkness, cast a muted glow on their tear-streaked faces. Among these grieving souls were Mary Magdalene, whose life had been utterly transformed by Jesus, and Mary, the mother of James and Joses, a woman whose dedication never wavered. Their hearts ached, and their sobs became the mournful soundtrack to the harrowing scene before them.

As the day's traumatic events began to draw to a close and the setting sun painted the horizon in melancholy hues, a lone figure approached with purposeful strides. Joseph of Arimathea, a man of wealth and influence, yet a secret disciple of Jesus, made his way to Pilate. With a courage that many lacked, he requested the body of Jesus. It was an audacious act; aligning oneself with a crucified man was fraught with peril. But for Joseph, honoring his Lord superseded all personal risks.

Pilate, perhaps surprised by this unexpected act of devotion, granted the request. With reverent hands, Joseph took the lifeless body of Jesus, wrapped it in clean linen, and laid it in his own new tomb, a resting place originally intended for himself. As the heavy stone was rolled to seal the tomb's entrance, the muted sounds of weeping echoed in the evening air. The world had just witnessed an honorable act, a testament to the profound impact Jesus had on those who truly knew Him.

Sealing the Tomb: The Leaders' Last Stand

The air was thick with an unsettling stillness a Jerusalem's sunset bathed the city in a fiery orange hue. Those mourning Jesus carried heavy hearts, their cries echoing through narrow streets, harmonizing with the fading day. Yet, amid this overwhelming grief, another group was stirring, motivated by a mixture of fear and determination.

The Pharisees and chief priests, despite their outward show of triumph, were plagued by an unsettling memory. They recalled Jesus' audacious claim that He would rise after three days. The very thought sent shivers down their spines. They had succeeded in crucifying Him, but the idea that His words might come true was a threat they couldn't ignore. Their victory, they felt, was incomplete as long as that prophecy lingered in the air.

In the waning light, they approached Pilate, their faces taut with anxiety. They expressed their concerns, their words betraying a hint of desperation. They secured a guard, not just any guard, but a Roman detail known for its discipline and efficiency. And as they sealed the stone, it wasn't just to keep intruders out, but to trap the prophecy inside, to make certain Jesus'

disciples couldn't forge a resurrection by stealing His body.

Yet, for all their efforts, the tomb, bathed now in moonlight, stood as a silent rebuke. The massive stone, the Roman seal, the elite guards — all these seemed trivial, almost laughable, against the backdrop of the universe's grand design. The religious leaders might have felt they were taking their last stand against Jesus and His teachings, but in reality, they were merely setting the stage for the most significant event in human history.

The city's usual Passover jubilations were over-shadowed by these events. As the last rays of light dis-appeared over Jerusalem, the city found itself on the edge of destiny, suspended between despair and hope, death and life. The next chapter in the divine drama was about to begin, and all of creation waited with bated breath.

CHAPTER 28

DAWN OF A NEW ERA

The Ultimate Conquest: Death's Stranglehold Broken

In the abyss of Hades, shadows of despair loomed. Satan, the prince of darkness, gloated over his seeming victory. For eons, he had held the keys of death, delighting in every soul he ensnared. But a sudden disturbance rippled through the netherworld. A brilliant light pierced the darkness, and with an authority unmatched, Jesus, the Anointed One, approached. With divine might, He wrested the keys from Satan's grasp. The old serpent's reign was shattered. The grip of death, the consequence of mankind's betrayal in Eden's garden, had been broken. The Savior had reclaimed what was rightfully His, preparing to rise and herald a new dawn for humanity.

The Resurrection:
Dawn's First Light Breaks the Night

The ancient city of Jerusalem lay blanketed in an uneasy silence. Streets that once teemed with the clamor of merchants and pilgrims now whispered tales of a crucified rabbi. As the first rays of dawn began to break, two women, Mary Magdalene and the other Mary, made their way toward the tomb. Their hearts, heavy with grief, yearned for a final glimpse of their beloved teacher.

The weather was cold, with a dampness that seeped into bones and souls alike. A thin mist floated above the ground, rendering everything slightly ethereal. Birds had yet to sing their morning songs, making the world feel suspended in time.

But as they approached, the earth trembled with an intensity that mirrored the quake of three days prior. An angel, radiant as lightning and clothed in garments white as snow, descended from the heavens. Rolling away the massive stone that sealed the tomb, he perched atop it, a divine sentinel.

The guards, trained Roman soldiers, hardened and battle-worn, trembled in terror. They were rendered as lifeless as stone, their bravado evaporating before the celestial messenger.

"Do not be afraid," the angel proclaimed, his voice kind yet powerful. He directed his words to the women, offering them comfort in their distress. "For I know that you seek Jesus, who was crucified. He is not here; for He is risen, as He said. Come, see the place where the Lord lay."

With bated breath, the women peered into the tomb, finding it empty. Their despair started to turn into hope, a fragile spark ready to ignite.

Hastening away, joy and fear intermingling in their hearts, they sought to deliver the miraculous news to the disciples. But on their way, an even more wondrous encounter awaited them. Jesus Himself, the Eternal One, the I AM, met them. "Greetings!" He called, His voice warm and familiar.

Instinctively, the women fell at His feet, their hands reaching out to touch the hem of His garment, as they once did during His earthly ministry. Tears of joy and relief streamed down their faces as they worshipped Him, their Savior and Friend.

"Do not be afraid," Jesus echoed the angel's earlier assurance. "Go and tell My brothers to go to Galilee, and there they will see Me."

The world, in that moment, teetered on the edge of a new era. The Savior had risen, and with His resurrection came the promise of eternal life for all who would believe. The dawn of hope had truly broken the night.

Shadows Whisper:
A Web of Deceit

As the sun ascended higher in the Jerusalem sky, casting its golden warmth upon the ancient city's stones, another narrative, much darker, began to weave itself in the corridors of power.

The soldiers who had been stationed at the tomb, their armor still resonating with the tremors of the earth and the celestial vision they had witnessed, hurriedly made their way to the city's religious elite. With each hurried step, their armor clinked, and the weight of the tale they bore grew heavier. Their minds raced, struggling to piece together the unbelievable events they had witnessed.

In the cold, dimly lit chambers of the Sanhedrin, the air thick with the scent of old scrolls and burning lamps, these battle-hardened soldiers relayed their account to the chief priests. The room, filled with the whispered rustling of robes and the nervous shifting of sandaled feet, hung on every word.

There, among the highest echelons of religious authority, a decision had to be made. The truth of the risen Savior posed a threat to their power, a chink in their meticulously constructed armor of control. For if the populace were to believe in this resurrection, the carefully laid foundations of their dominion would crumble.

With hushed voices and darting glances, they conspired. Silver coins gleamed as they exchanged hands, the price for silence and falsehood. "Say that His disciples came by night and stole Him away while we were asleep," they whispered to the soldiers, their voices dripping with a mix of desperation and authority.

But the soldiers, men of honor despite their flaws, hesitated. "How can we claim to have slept through such an event?" they protested. "Our very duty was to guard, and now we speak of sleep?"

The chief priests, seasoned in the art of manipulation, replied cunningly, "Should this come to the governor's ears, we will satisfy him and keep you out of trouble."

And so, a false narrative was birthed. A story of deceit that sought to overshadow the brilliance of the resurrection. As the soldiers left, their pockets heavier but spirits burdened, the chief priests looked upon each other with a mix of relief and anxiety. They had, for the moment, secured their worldly status, but in the depths of their souls, the truth echoed, unstoppable.

Outside, the world remained unchanged, yet within the hearts of those who knew the truth, a flame of hope burned bright. The shadows might whisper, but they could never extinguish the light.

The Mountainside Epiphany: When Faith Met Doubt

The air was different in Galilee. Away from the stifling heat and turmoil of Jerusalem, the gentle breeze carried whispers of ancient tales and legends. Here, among the verdant hills and tranquil waters, the disciples were summoned. A rendezvous set by the risen Messiah himself.

As they approached the designated mountain, memories flooded their minds—of miracles performed, lessons imparted, and prophecies foretold. The path, though familiar, felt entirely new, charged with anticipation.

Upon reaching the crest, a silhouette awaited them, bathed in the golden glow of the setting sun. It was Him—their teacher, their friend, their Savior. The reality of His presence was overwhelming. No grave could contain Him; no stone could hold Him back.

Driven by a divine magnetism, they drew close, their hearts pounding in their chests. And then, as recognition dawned, as the weight of the reality settled, most fell to their knees, overwhelmed. Their hands reached out to touch the ground before Him, their foreheads pressed to the earth. This was not merely homage to a revered teacher; this was worship to the Son of the Living God. The gravity of who Jesus truly was crystallized in that moment—a revelation more profound than any they had experienced before.

Yet, amidst this congregation of the faithful, there were hushed whispers of uncertainty. Doubtful glances exchanged between furrowed brows. Some

wondered if their eyes betrayed them. Could it be an illusion? A spectral manifestation of their collective grief and longing? Perhaps a mirage brought about by the desert's cruel sun?

And among them stood Thomas, the ever-skeptical, ever-questing disciple. His gaze, intense and searching, lingered on Jesus. The raw pain of recent loss was still fresh, the wound of unbelief still open. He had declared his need for undeniable proof before, a tactile testament to believe the unbelievable. And yet, here he stood, on the precipice of faith, wrestling with a hope so potent it was terrifying.

The atmosphere was thick with an electric mix of reverence and tension, faith, and doubt. On this mountainside, at this divine intersection, destinies would be shaped, and the trajectory of humanity forever altered.

The Proclamation of Authority:
When Heaven and Earth Bowed

The silence on the mountainside was palpable, broken only by the soft rustle of the breeze and the labored breaths of the disciples, each consumed by their own turmoil of emotion. Then, Jesus stepped forward, His robes billowing gently around Him. His gaze, filled with a depth of wisdom and eternity, surveyed the horizon and then settled intently upon the group.

The disciples instinctively felt a shift in the air. It was as if the very earth beneath them trembled in

recognition of the authority of the One who stood before them.

"All power," He began, His voice echoing with the weight of ages, "is given unto me in heaven and in earth."

The disciples were transported back to a different time, to the beginning when the first man and woman, created in God's image, were entrusted with dominion over all creation. The Garden of Eden, where a treacherous deceit led to mankind relinquishing that authority to the cunning serpent, Satan. The world had since been held captive under the dark dominion of the deceiver.

Recollections of Jesus' time in the wilderness, fasting for forty days and nights, played out in their minds. How Satan had come to Him, attempting to bargain, offering the kingdoms of the world—a dominion he had stolen. But Jesus had resisted, maintaining His purity, His mission undeterred.

And now, here on this mountainside, it all came full circle. The second Adam, untainted and triumphant, stood reclaiming what had been lost. The treason of Eden was undone. The grip of Satan shattered. The rightful heir had returned, and with Him, He brought the promise of restoration.

Tears streamed down Peter's face as he grasped the enormity of what was unfolding. Mary Magdalene's heart raced, memories of her own deliverance from darkness at the hands of Jesus flooding her mind. John, the beloved disciple, looked up with a mix of awe and understanding, realizing that the ultimate sacrifice had paved the way for this very moment.

All of creation seemed to pause, acknowledging the shift in the cosmic order. Jesus had not only defeated death but had also wrested back authority from the prince of this world. He was the bridge between heaven and earth, and through Him, humanity could once again walk in the authority and dominion they were always intended to have.

The weight of His words lingered in the air, a testament to the unshakeable authority and power of the Eternal One, the I AM. The past's shadows were dispelled, and a new era of hope and promise dawned.

The Great Commission: Humanity's Rediscovered Purpose

The landscape was bathed in a golden hue, the setting sun casting elongated shadows that danced with the whispers of the wind. The disciples, still caught in the gravity of Jesus' proclamation of authority, now felt a stirring in their spirits, as if they were on the cusp of something monumental.

Jesus' gaze, so recently filled with the immense gravity of cosmic authority, now softened with a tender, paternal affection. He stepped closer, and they could feel His love enveloping them, reminding them of the countless times they had seen Him heal the sick, feed the hungry, and cast out demons.

"Go ye therefore," He began, His voice layered with the weight of destiny, "and teach all nations, baptizing them in the name of the Father, and of the Son, and of the Holy Ghost."

Images flashed before the disciples' eyes. Of vast lands beyond their own, of peoples of every tribe and tongue. Of seas to be crossed, mountains to be climbed, and valleys to be traversed. A world awaiting the message of hope and redemption. They realized that they were not merely being asked; they were being commissioned. Entrusted with the greatest mission ever known to man.

The profundity of the task was not lost on them. They remembered their own baptism, the overwhelming sensation of being immersed in water, only to emerge transformed, reborn. And now, they were to be the vessels, carrying forth the promise of this rebirth to every corner of the earth.

"Teaching them," Jesus continued, His voice now firm with determination, "to observe all things whatsoever I have commanded you."

Memories of their time with Jesus flooded back— the parables, the lessons, the miracles. The Sermon on the Mount, the raising of Lazarus, the feeding of the five thousand. Every moment, every word, was a treasure to be shared, a beacon of light for a world groping in darkness.

John felt a shiver run down his spine. Mary's hands clenched into fists, filled with a newfound purpose. Peter, always the impulsive one, looked ready to start at that very moment, the fire of passion burning in his eyes.

"And lo," Jesus' voice dropped to a gentle whisper, causing everyone to lean in, "I am with you always, even unto the end of the world."

The magnitude of His promise settled over them. They would not be alone. Even in their most challenging moments, in the face of peril, persecution, or pain, the presence of the I AM would be their guiding light. The Eternal One, who had bridged heaven and earth, would be their constant companion.

As the last rays of the sun dipped below the horizon, casting the world into twilight, a sense of profound purpose fused the group together. They were no longer just followers; they were ambassadors, carriers of the most significant message the world had ever known. And with the authority and power of Heaven behind them, they would change the course of history.

THE END

STORY CONTINUES IN THE BOOK OF ACTS

EPILOGUE:

ECHOES THROUGH TIME

As the sun set on that momentous chapter in history, the world, unbeknownst to many, had irrevocably changed. The words and actions of Jesus, a carpenter from the modest town of Nazareth, reverberated through the valleys and across the hills, permeating hearts and minds, challenging norms, and reshaping destinies.

Jesus' message was simple, yet profound – love, forgiveness, sacrifice, and redemption. But it wasn't just the content of His teachings that captivated souls; it was the embodiment of these principles in His life, death, and resurrection. In Jesus, humanity saw not just a teacher or a prophet, but the living manifestation of God's love and mercy.

The events that transpired in Jerusalem, culminating in the resurrection, were just the beginning. From the cobbled streets of Judea to the grandeur of Rome, from the desert sands of Africa to the icy fjords of Scandinavia, the message spread like wildfire. It ignit-

ed a movement that, over millennia, would grow into a global community bound together by faith, hope, and love.

The stories recounted in this book are more than just historical events. They are a testament to the indomitable spirit of truth that, once unleashed, can never be suppressed. They serve as a beacon of hope to the weary, a balm to the wounded, and a call to action for the complacent.

Even today, as the world faces unprecedented challenges, the teachings of Jesus remain as relevant as ever. They beckon us towards unity, compassion, and understanding, urging us to transcend our differences and recognize the divine spark in every soul.

So, as we close this chapter and reflect on the life and teachings of Jesus, let's remember that His story doesn't end here. It continues in each one of us, in the choices we make, the love we share, and the hope we instill. In embracing His message, we join a timeless symphony of believers, echoing Jesus' profound truths through the annals of time.

AFTERWORD:

THE TIMELESSNESS OF TRUTH

The creation of this narrative, deeply inspired by the book of Matthew, was both a literary and spiritual endeavor. This book sought to expand upon and bring to life the cherished stories within Matthew, aiming to stay as close and accurate to the original narrative as possible. The tales, though ancient, are imbued with universal truths that have shaped civilizations and personal faiths for centuries.

While set in a time and place far removed from our modern world, these stories consistently reminded me of their eternal relevance. In every age—whether ancient, modern, or somewhere in between—the lessons and virtues exemplified by Jesus and His disciples shine as guiding beacons.

Our current digital, high-speed age often places immediate satisfaction over enduring virtues such as patience, understanding, and love. Yet, in the pages of Matthew, and its heartfelt retelling here, we find a poignant reminder of the undying importance of these virtues.

Our advancements in technology haven't negated our fundamental human desires for connection, purpose, and redemption. The core human dilemmas of identity, meaning, and belonging remain. Through this narrative, which expands upon the life and teachings of Jesus as presented in Matthew, I hope readers find resonating answers to these timeless questions.

To you, the reader, it's my sincere wish that this book has been more than a riveting tale. I hope it has provided a moment of reflection, a chance to contemplate your beliefs, values, and purpose. Jesus' message, while rooted in a specific time and religion, transcends boundaries and epochs, urging us all towards compassion, integrity, and an unwavering faith in love's transformative power.

In closing, a saying often attributed to various historical figures comes to mind: "The more things change, the more they stay the same." In the ageless teachings of Jesus, as portrayed in Matthew and retold here, we discover enduring wisdom for every change, every challenge, and every chapter of our lives.

RESOURCES

Find upcoming books and media publish
by Rekindle Publish.

WWW.REKINDLEPUBLISH.COM

Find us on Social Media!

TikTok - @rekindlepublish
Facebook - @rekindlenetwork

Contact us

info@rekindlepublish.com

For publishing inquiries

publish@rekindlepublish.com

W W W . R E K I N D L E P U B L I S H . C O M

COMING SOON

The Servant's Odyssey:
Retelling the Gospel of Mark
Coming Spring 2024

www.ingramcontent.com/pod-product-compliance
Lightning Source LLC
Chambersburg PA
CBHW031202010826
48971CB00013B/1216